The Lies of Saints

**Books by Sigmund Brouwer
from Tyndale House Publishers**

Pony Express Christmas
The Leper
Out of the Shadows
Crown of Thorns

SIGMUND

THE
LIES
OF
SAINTS

A
NICK BARRETT
MYSTERY

BROUWER

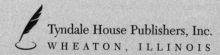
Tyndale House Publishers, Inc.
WHEATON, ILLINOIS

Visit Tyndale's exciting Web site at www.tyndale.com

The Lies of Saints

Edited by James H. Cain III and Ramona Cramer Tucker

Designed by Catherine Bergstrom

Scripture quotations are taken from the *Holy Bible,* New Living Translation, copyright © 1996. Used by permission of Tyndale House Publishers, Inc., Wheaton, Illinois 60189. All rights reserved.

Library of Congress Cataloging-in-Publication Data

Brouwer, Sigmund, date.
  The lies of the saints / Sigmund Brouwer.
    p. cm.
  ISBN 0-8423-6594-X (sc)
    1. Citadel, the Military College of South Carolina—Fiction. 2. Military education—Fiction. 3. Charleston (S.C.)—Fiction. 4. College students—Fiction. 5. Hazing—Fiction. I. Title.
  PS3552.R6825L54 2003
  813'.54—dc21
                                          2003007989

Printed in the United States of America

09 08 07 06 05 04 03
8   7   6   5   4   3   2   1

With much love,
for my mother,
Gerda

✛

You can enter God's Kingdom

only through the narrow gate.

The highway to hell is broad,

and its gate is wide for the many

who choose the easy way.

But the gateway to life is small,

and the road is narrow,

and only a few ever find it.

Matthew 7:13-14

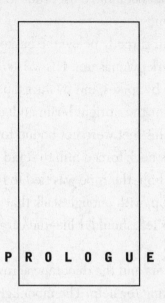

PROLOGUE

A shaft of moonlight from the gymnasium's upper window speared the solitary figure of Anson Hanoway Saffron and threw onto the hardwood floor the sharp shadow of the cross that held him captive.

Anson Hanoway Saffron was seventeen, a first-year cadet at the Citadel, South Carolina's famed military college. He had entered the hallowed school in September with the burden of expectations that went with his name and heritage. As a further detriment, he was slim and quiet and gentle and sensitive—a terrible combination of traits for anyone to bring into a military training institute.

He'd endured five months, ten days, and roughly twelve · hours at the Citadel since he'd waved good-bye to his mother at the gates and first stepped onto the grounds. The last half

hour of his time at the Citadel had been the most brutal . . .
leading to this, a mock crucifixion.

He'd been placed on a chair directly below the basketball net, at the far end of the dark gymnasium. His wrists
were held to the crossbeam not by spikes, but by duct tape.
His feet supported his weight, for the upright beam ended
just above his ankles. Although his feet were not bound to the
cross, a rope knotted around his neck forced him to stand
motionless on the chair. Above him, the rope was tied to the
base of the metal basketball hoop, with enough slack that
a small length of it rested on his left shoulder like the caress
of a snake.

He wore only a pair of boxers and the duct tape across
his mouth to keep him from crying for help. The moonlight
showed his adolescent skin was smooth of hair. But not of
smears of green and red paint.

In front of the chair, in the darkness beneath that shaft
of moonlight, stood four of the Citadel's finest seniors. Their
faces were hidden by black balaclava masks, and their squared
shoulders showed the satisfaction of a job well done.

To place him on the chair, the four seniors had worked
silently and smoothly, like a perfectly planned military maneu-
ver. Their silence had been broken only by the slapping of
their soft-heeled shoes against the hardwood of the gymnasium
floor and by the plopping of excess paint that slid off the
brushes onto the boy's body and then onto the floor.

As the seniors allowed themselves their brief satisfaction,
a distant rattle came from the boiler-room pipes. When the
rattle ended, the only other clear sound in the gymnasium

came from Anson Hanoway Saffron, as the air of his rapid breaths whistled faintly through his nostrils.

"It's not too late," whispered one of the four. "You know what we want from you. Just nod. That's all it will take. And we'll let you down."

"One simple nod," a second one said. "And we'll make sure that no senior touches you."

"Nothing like this will ever happen to you again," the third one whispered. "You'll be one of us."

"We'll become your protectors," the last one added. "Just nod. That's all we need from you. Then we'll understand you've made the right choice."

Anson Hanoway Saffron stared straight ahead. Tears began to trickle down his cheeks like tiny balls of mercury in the silver of the moonlight.

"That's it, then," the first cadet said. "We have our answer."

Each of the fine senior cadets gave Anson Hanoway Saffron a mock salute. Then, as one man, the four seniors turned and marched away in precise formation.

Anson knew who they were; the masks merely ensured he couldn't positively identify them to the authorities. Nor would he be able to tell anyone he had recognized any by their voices. In the time that it had taken to remove him from his dormitory room and prepare him like this beneath the net, none of the four seniors had spoken to the freshman in more than a whisper.

When they'd first burst through his door and surprised him on his knees at prayer beside his bed, they'd used whispers to tell him what they were going to do and why. Unless he gave them what they wanted.

Now as they left him alone to hang from the cross in silence, the seniors had no need to whisper again. They knew soon enough that their victim would understand how much they hated him. And all he stood for.

Anson Hanoway Saffron discovered how well they had done their work. He was unable to move from the chair.

If he tried to jump, the rope tied around his neck was too short for him to reach the floor with his feet. Nor, with his hands taped to the crossbeam, could he remove the rope around his neck.

That meant he would have to remain standing on the chair the entire night, waiting for the gymnasium door to open in the morning. Waiting for parents to stream in for the first basketball game of the weekend's tournament.

That left him the other choice.

To avoid the humiliation, he could kick the chair out from underneath him and let them find him hanging on his cross, his eyes deadened of any soul.

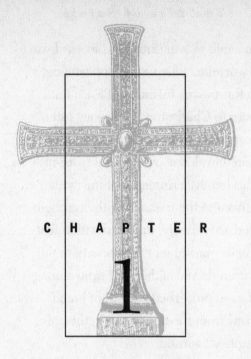

CHAPTER
1

I was born Nicholas Thomas Barrett, and I grew up in an antebellum mansion in the world south of Broad Street, an east-west street that separates the barbarians north of it from Charleston's aristocracy, including my family of fifth-generation Charlestonians.

I, however, did not have a privileged childhood.

My mother, a waitress in a diner who looked like she had stepped out of an old-fashioned Coca-Cola poster, married into this elite family much to their disapproval. This disapproval was never spoken, but day after day she faced the menace of their silence. To them, she finally proved their judgment correct when I was born just after the beginning of the Vietnam War, long after nine months had passed since the departure of her husband for training and the early stages of the war, where he would die as a military hero.

Naturally, their disdain spilled over onto me, born as I was in and of sin. My situation worsened when, to all appearances, my mother abandoned me for reasons I would not learn until decades later upon my return to Charleston after a long exile. With her departure in the summer of my tenth birthday, I essentially became an orphan—an unwelcome responsibility for my dead father's brother and his family, a reminder of my mother's lack of character, and an affront to the memory of the war hero she'd betrayed. I was treated accordingly, so I lived within that menace of silence, an insidious punishment far worse than the occasional beating that I suffered. And, although I lived among the extremely wealthy, not even proverbial crumbs of bread were permitted to fall my way from the family meals; the only pocket money I held was money I earned.

During my early teens, I was desperate to escape as often as possible the mansion that was my prison then and, ironically, is now my home. In those years, I would walk north of Broad, lie about my name, and work any odd job that would allow me to squirrel away enough money to eventually purchase a replacement bicycle for the one that my uncle had taken away from me in the summer my mother disappeared. This new bicycle made it easier to continue to go north of Broad in search of odd jobs. There was a spot near the yacht club where I chained and locked that bicycle every day before walking the last few blocks to the Barrett mansion. I knew well that if I ever appeared at the mansion with the bicycle, it would have raised too many questions.

The work to earn it and the subterfuge to keep it, however, were well compensated by the freedom the heavy, fat-tired Schwinn gave me. When I wasn't working, I roamed all of the boroughs of old Charleston.

I was often drawn to the square bungalows of the neighborhood near the Citadel. The Citadel is the almost sacred military school whose cadets fired the first shots of the Civil War. It is a place where generation upon generation of Charleston's elite have sent their sons to prove themselves. Those who graduate form an unspoken private club impervious to the opinion of the rest of the world.

Looking back, I believe I was drawn to the institution by longing and hatred. Longing first, because I knew the Citadel was destiny for many of the boys south of Broad, including my cousin Pendleton, older than me and living in the mansion with his father and mother, while I was the ignored outsider at the family meals. It seemed to me that becoming a Citadel graduate would give me respect in Charleston.

Yet often I hated it more passionately than I longed for it to become part of my own destiny. In my early years I'd believed the soldier my mother had married was indeed my father, and because of it had swelled with pride whenever the Citadel was mentioned. But the summer my mother left was also the summer I discovered I was illegitimate, and I would not discover for decades who had fathered me. Along with all my cherished misconceptions about my identity went the sense of ownership, the Citadel pride, swept away with nearly everything else that was important to me.

Since it was made clear to me that I, unlike Pendleton, would never attend the Citadel, it was a defense mechanism to hate the two Citadel possessions I had lost—pride in the school of a father and a chance to be part of the tradition myself.

During the afternoons, however, when the longing for it was greater than my hatred, I would drift on my Schwinn through the neighborhoods around the Citadel.

I envied the seemingly happy families I found there, their contentment worth far more than the isolated, cold hatred that filled the spectacular Barrett mansion, within easy riding distance but another world away. On those quiet streets, I would see mothers pushing carriages or strollers. I often watched, from a distance, other boys my age so engaged in games of street baseball that they didn't notice my yearning to be invited into their unrehearsed joy. I would see, too, men in sleeveless undershirts sitting on the porches, sweating out the late-afternoon heat with bottles of Dr. Pepper in their hands. I envied, too, that liberty. Where I grew up, sweat or sleeveless undershirts in public, or consumption of a beverage not served in a glass by a black maid was each considered verging on scandalous—the combination of all three was unthinkable. And cutting into this neighborhood was Hampton Park, for all practical purposes an extension of the Citadel. It was acres and acres of quiet paths among giant oaks, manicured lawns, and serene ponds. The same place, I found out later, that drew another young man the way the water of the ponds drew deer on foggy mornings.

Anson Hanoway Saffron.

I was just past forty years of age when Anson Hanoway Saffron first spoke to me. This was long after his death, but his poignant words crossed time and space to reach me. This, I believe, is one

of the greatest human accomplishments. That the abstract
symbols of the alphabet can construct words that form pictures,
and that these pictures made of words can speak across centuries
and miles. So that when, for example, I read *The Jewish Wars*,
the voice of Josephus speaks to me as plainly as if he and I were
in the same room, and I relive with him the great tragedies of
one of the most tumultuous decades in world history.

Anson Hanoway Saffron's diary, of course, held none of the
importance to the rest of the world of any the great narrators
throughout the centuries, nor did he write a work that would be
published or celebrated. He wrote to please himself, in a journal.
This same journal—a leather-bound diary of thick, parchment
pages, with precise handwriting showing the whirls and blobs of
a fountain pen—eventually reached me. It was easy to guess that
his gentle, romanticized view of the world included the need to
avoid something as modern and convenient as a ballpoint.
Although close to thirty years had passed since he'd written his
diary entries, his obvious bewilderment and innocence and
yearning were not lessened by the passage of time.

This was his journal entry for December 15. At fifteen, he
would enter the Citadel in September of the following year,
and so would begin the chain of events that would lead to his
death.

I am human, and I know I will die.
These are the words that keep running through my
head as I lie awake at night.
I am human, and I know I will die.

Isn't that a curse? I don't think animals live with the
knowledge that someday they'll die. I bet they just exist
in each moment, chasing food or running away from
being food for other animals, never aware that each day
that passes is another day closer to their deaths.

I am human. I will die.

Maybe that's why people do animal things—so they
can block that out of their heads. I see my parents and
their friends and how they act. Eat and drink and be
merry, for tomorrow is another day to eat and drink
and be merry. Who can think about dying when they're
busy eating and drinking and being merry?

But it takes courage not to live that way. If I could
pray, that's what I would ask for. Courage to hope and
dream and love someone even though I know that death
will someday take them away from me.

I am human, and I know I will die. But I will face
death with courage. Is that how I can define myself if I
don't want to be Anson Hanoway Saffron, the son of the
father? The boy who is supposed to follow the family's
traditions?

I feel so alone. Maybe that's what it means to be
human. To feel separated and alone. Sometimes I
wonder what it would be like to meet the right girl and

have her fall in love with me as much as I fall in love with her. Then I realize that no matter how close I might get to her, and no matter how close she might get to me, and no matter how much we love each other forever, I can't become part of her and she can't become part of me. We will still be separate humans. Always. All we can be is two alone people together. And that maybe will ease the aloneness, but each of us will still be alone.

I am human, and I know I will die. I will die alone.

Even if I have a wife and lots of kids and grandkids and even if they are gathered at my bed as I draw my last breath, I will still be alone, going by myself to the other side. Whatever that is. Wherever that is.

I guess then I will find out if I have a soul.

If I don't, what is there to question? I should just be Anson Hanoway Saffron, the son of his father. And I should eat, drink, and be merry like him and have a boy to carry on the family name, to become the son of his father and carry on the family traditions.

But what if I do have a soul? Why? How? Maybe that's the purpose of a human. To search for those answers.

I am human. I will die.

I doubt as he wrote those words that Anson Hanoway Saffron expected to die because of the Citadel. But then how many of us have the luxury of seeing the approach of our own death, the luxury of enough warning to decide the important matters of why we have a soul and where it will go?

He, at least, was asking the questions that each of us must.

✛

I was thirteen years old in the fall that Anson Hanoway Saffron entered the Citadel.

Although I would have recognized his name—south of Broad is essentially a cloistered community—I did not know him by acquaintance. Did not know yet that he and I had solitude in common, each for our different reasons. Did not know yet his fondness for the open spaces and generous quiet of Hampton Park because of his desperate need for seclusion.

Did not know yet about his one fateful evening there.

Because old Charleston seems immune to time, that evening would have been the same as any early September evening now, with the air just before sunset so calm and still that the cadences from the Citadel vibrated from a distance; the long shadows so sharp and the light so tinged with substance that it was like walking into a landscape painting.

Perhaps that evening, on the bicycle I took pride in oiling so well that it was a silent ghost slipping through the lives of others, I passed Anson Hanoway Saffron. Maybe he was deep in his own thoughts as he walked down one of the park's many paths, unaware of how that night would intersect with my life so many years later.

I was fortunate; my evening in the park changed nothing in my adolescent life.

For Anson Hanoway Saffron, however, that beautiful September night in Hampton Park would haunt and mark him, just as surely as his horrific night on the cross in the Citadel's gymnasium would alter and destroy the lives of too many others around him.

And then, much later, mark mine too.

C H A P T E R

2

Two or three heartbeats. Not much time to comprehend the approach of death. Yet far too long to be helplessly gripping a steering wheel, staring into the rearview mirror at the hood and grille and headlights of a truck—four tons of engine and rubber and steel—bearing down at a velocity of eighty miles an hour, one hundred and seventeen feet per second.

Two or three heartbeats. Barely enough time for my friend Kellie Mixson to be engulfed by the roar of comprehending disbelief, to be clutched by breath-stopping cold. Time enough for regret and fear, to wish for more time. And then all was shattered by the crash of metal and glass.

Her scream of terror was lost in the shriek of metal against metal as the force of the truck's impact rammed the red

BMW through the stop sign and onto the highway into cross traffic. Front end knifed by a minivan. Spun sideways. Hit again by a Honda sedan from the other direction.

Drivers hit brakes in panic, but the screeching was lost in the thud of each impact until the BMW landed on its side and gouged the road as it slid to the shoulder. The spray of shards of windshield across the asphalt. Talcum powder of exploding air bags briefly misted above the road, then dispersed in an early evening breeze that smelled of the tang of the ocean.

Silence. Except for the diesel engines of the barges on the nearby river, going in and out of the port of Charleston, the hum of traffic across the high bridge that silhouetted the evening sky. Brief silence.

Then drivers up and down the highway, impatient with the delay and too far away to see the accident, began honking their horns. Eventually, the inevitable sirens cut the fall air . . . though Kellie was far, far beyond hearing them. Or the firemen cutting open the roof of her BMW. Or the grunts of the paramedics as they lifted her into the back of the ambulance.

This was the mercy granted to her. After those two or three heartbeats of comprehending disbelief at the sight of the truck in the rearview mirror, she knew nothing else until two days and three operations later, the day of her thirtieth birthday. Then pain pulsed into her consciousness—bursting through the barrier of hospital opiates like a tank through a sheet of paper—and gave Kellie the first clue that she was still alive.

"Nick."

This wing of the hospital had a television lounge, but the television was silent. An old man in a hospital gown stared out the window, hands behind his back, shoulders slouched. Angel and Maddie Starr sat on the sofa, facing the hallway. Angel was twelve, Maddie not quite two. At first glance they didn't look like sisters. Angel's skin was dusky, her eyes green. Maddie's skin was beautiful ebony, her eyes matching. When each smiled, however, they showed their resemblance to their mother; I had seen photos and video footage of her with them. Half sisters in blood, these two were more than sisters in love. I'd seen Angel's determination to give up her life, if necessary, for Maddie months earlier and admired her greatly for it.

Angel had been waiting for me in the television lounge. As she'd called my name, she had stood. Not smiling.

Instead of continuing down the hall to Kellie Mixson's room, I set down the computer bag she'd sent me to get from her office. It wasn't that heavy, but my lower right leg is a prosthesis, thanks to a car accident of my own. Carrying anything over five pounds is awkward for me, and the closest parking spot I'd been able to find wasn't that close.

"Nick," Angel repeated. Something in her voice worried me.

"Kellie," I said. "Is she . . . ?"

An hour earlier, I'd left Angel and Maddie in Kellie's room—Maddie in the bed with Kellie, studiously using crayons on a coloring book, and Angel in a chair beside the bed, reading aloud from *To Kill a Mockingbird.*

This had been the first chance for Kellie to receive visitors since the accident a week earlier. Her jaw was wired shut, and in a shaky mumble, she'd given me her office security code, asked me to get a file box, which was still in my Jeep, and her laptop. Kellie was a private eye who had entered my life at the same time as Angel. During my search for the truth about a misplaced antique painting that mysteriously appeared in Angel's hands decades after it had been stolen on the night of the murder of a Charleston aristocrat.

"Kellie? She's all right, Nick," Angel said in reply to my question.

Angel understood my concern without hearing me voice it. Angel knew that, until Kellie's accident, Kellie and I had spent daily workouts together at the gym and more than the occasional lunch in enjoyable conversation.

As the two girls approached, Maddie clung to Angel's right hand. In her left hand, Angel held Maddie's coloring book and the paperback copy of Harper Lee's fine novel about the South. Angel hadn't read much up to this point. Now that they had crossed Broad Street into my world, I hoped *To Kill a Mockingbird* would give us a way to discuss racism without making it seem like a personal issue. After all, we lived in the South, and racism hadn't ended with emancipation or Martin Luther King Jr. Since I knew it was inevitable that Angel had experienced racism already and that she was smart enough to eventually guess this was the reason I'd given her the book, I'd made it seem like Kellie really wanted to hear the story to pass time in the hospital.

Angel handed it to me. "Page thirty-five."

It had been too long since I'd read it myself. I wondered what on that page had disturbed Angel enough to send her out of Kellie's room to wait for me here with Maddie. I opened the novel to where Angel had dog-eared it.

Kellie had written in red crayon across the page in hasty block letters: *N. u work 4 me. plz.*

"Tell me what happened," I said. "When did she write this? Why?"

"Five minutes ago. I was reading to Kellie. A man in a suit came in the room. He told me to leave. Didn't ask. *Told* me. I said I was there to help Kellie. Kellie took the book from my hand and pointed for me to take Maddie. When I was reaching over Kellie, she pulled on the front of my shirt and I fell. It must have hurt Kellie bad because I landed on her hips where the doctors put on a cast. So I was saying sorry and trying to get Maddie and the coloring book and the crayons. Kellie must have wrote in the book during the confusion 'cause when she handed it back to me it was open to that page. Then she shut it fast so the man couldn't read what she wrote. She means you, right, Nick? But you don't work for her. She's a private investigator. You don't have a job."

"Thanks, Angel," I said dryly. "No, I am not employed." I was on an extended sabbatical from a job teaching astronomy at a community college.

"And yes," I continued, "I would guess she wrote this note for me. Who was the man?"

"I don't like him. He was like Robert Ewell."

"Robert Ewell?"

"You know. In the book, Nick, the man who lived behind a garbage dump in Maycomb. The one that Scout's daddy Atticus stood up to in the trial."

I squinted.

"I already read the book. Last night when you gave it to me and said Kellie would love to hear me read it. But how could you know if you hadn't seen Kellie yet since the accident? So it made me wonder why you were making such a big deal about the book. And now I know. You don't think I already met people like that? They're so stupid it doesn't bother me. Much."

"Angel?"

"I didn't like this guy in Kellie's room. The one like Robert Ewell. I took Maddie off Kellie's bed in case he tried to hurt Maddie. But I wasn't going to leave Kellie alone with him. You told me to take care of her while you were gone getting the computer. So I put Maddie in my lap and tried to stay. Maybe I shouldn't have told him that the only way he was going to get me out of the room was by throwing me out. That man grabbed me by the neck, squeezed hard enough that it hurt, pulled Maddie and me out of the room, and slammed the door. Called us stupid kids. Except it wasn't kids he called us. He used another word, Nick. It's the only word I hate. Especially for someone to call Maddie by that name."

I didn't have to ask.

She whispered it to me anyway, her beautiful face screwed up with sadness and anger.

"He still with Kellie?" I asked, the ugly racism tearing at my gut.

Angel nodded.

"I'd like you and Maddie to wait here in the television room until I get back," I said. "Could you do that for me?"

"I don't like the look on your face, Nick. It makes me afraid for you, like you might do something real stupid in there. He's bigger than you."

"Angel . . ."

"Worse than that, he's got a gun."

C H A P T E R

3

I'd first met Angel a few months earlier, in the emergency department of this very hospital. Angel had brought Maddie in with a fever. She was so desperate to make sure a doctor cared for her sister that, armed with only a ballpoint pen, she had managed to take hostage a bullying security guard twice her size.

As a bystander, I'd stepped in and made arrangements both to help the security guard and to ensure that Maddie would see a doctor.

The disappearance of Angel's grandmother and other events in the week that followed drew me further into Angel's life. At week's end, when it became apparent that she and Maddie might fall into the abyss of the social welfare system, I had volunteered to become their guardian.

It wasn't a difficult thing to do. And now I couldn't imagine life without them.

Angel had charm and charisma and far more: she had a determination to reach beyond what life had dealt her. Her mother and grandmother had raised her well; this legacy was worth far more than the money and small house that had been left to her. And this money she had already set aside before she came to live with me; she received only a small allowance until she was eighteen. Angel, unlike most girls her age, was so afraid she might not be able to support Maddie that money was something to be hoarded like food in a famine. As Angel had been taught to look ahead, she devoted much of her considerable intelligence to understanding the computer world; it was her ticket to freedom.

As for me, I had a legacy of my own. I'd recently inherited the Barrett family mansion and a substantial trust fund that had resulted from finding out the identity of my father upon my return to Charleston. That meant having the two of them enter my life was not much of a sacrifice—in finance or time. And yet, being a guardian held responsibilities I was determined to take as seriously as if I were their father. I prayed daily for the wisdom to fulfill my role.

I'd immediately hired live-in housekeepers to provide stability and respectability, and all of us had settled into an enjoyable routine. All told, I felt I had received the better part of the bargain with the privilege of Angel and Maddie as additions to my life.

When I accepted my role as guardian, I'd expected there might be times, particularly since we lived in the South, when the color of their skin would bring difficulties into our shared life. But I had also discovered, throughout my life, that racism is not unique to the South. It can take many forms— including the menacing silence that had scarred my early teens.

Indeed, I believe overt racism is far easier to fight, for it is at least a visible foe.

And something that can be resisted.

Civilly or not.

So that day, still hearing the echoes of the single word that Angel had whispered into my ear, I walked into the hospital room, hands empty and heart filled with cold rage.

Angel had been right about the gun. It was an indication of her upbringing on the streets that she'd spotted it under the man's suit jacket. He wore it in a shoulder holster, the black straps and black gun metal a stark contrast to his white dress shirt.

He was sitting beside Kellie's bed. Just as Angel had said, he wore an expensive dark suit, with the jacket now hanging on the back of the chair. His blond hair was cut short and ragged and spiked, a style meant to disguise how the hair was thinning. Aside from the pistol in his holster, he seemed just like the suits you see in packs at the airport, traveling from one gate to another with other corporate clones, smug and secure in the identity they take from belonging to the top of the business food chain.

He surveyed me without any indication of friendliness. Perhaps I wasn't hiding my rage as well as I intended.

"This is Nick," Kellie told him, speaking slowly through her motionless jaw.

Although I'd spent a half hour with her upon first getting to the hospital, it still shocked me to see the damage the accident had done to her. One leg was suspended in a cast. Her hair had been shaved, and her face was mottled and swollen. Stitches covered her forehead in random patterns.

The man in the suit remained seated. "Good. Give me what you got on Sebastian."

I didn't answer. Wanted him to break the silence.

He did, about twenty seconds later. "What I'm wondering," he said to Kellie, "is why you never mentioned him before. Thought you worked alone."

"Kellie," I said, "you want him out of here? Just nod."

She grimaced but shook her head. "Nick, this is Miles Ashby. From the Chicago agency that hired us to look into Victoria Sebastian's disappearance."

I caught her emphasis on *us* and wondered why, suddenly, I was involved.

"I only answer to you," I told Kellie. So she would understand I'd read her crayon message. "No one else."

By then, Miles had stood in response to my implied threat. He was about an inch taller than my six feet. Ten pounds heavier, maybe 195. Ten years younger. And he wanted me to see it.

"Please," he said without smiling, "please try to move me out of this room. My therapist says I have a lot of buried hostility. Says I have a pinched soul, that I need to bring my anger out in the open. It'd give me a lot of pleasure to hurt you. Be good for my soul too."

I met his stare.

We were only a couple of feet apart. His hands hung loosely at his sides, as if he were ready for me to take a swing. I was tempted. It probably showed in my own body language. I can only guess how it looked to Angel as she and Maddie followed a female nurse into the room.

"Kellie," Angel called from the doorway, "I got help as fast as I could."

With the middle-aged nurse smiling politely, Angel spoke to me in a theatrical whisper. "It's the bedpan. I think it's full."

The bedpan was fine. Angel had just found an excuse to bring a third party into the room to prevent me from doing anything stupid. Like getting hurt.

I grinned inwardly. This kid knew me well.

"We'll step outside," Ashby said in a low voice. He pinched my elbow.

"If you don't let go," I said in an equally low voice, "it's going to get really ugly in here."

He dropped his hand, which gave me a small measure of satisfaction. He stepped past me and out into the hallway.

I moved to Kellie and leaned over. It hurt to see how battered and helpless she was. "Just so I understand, you're working for him, and I'm working for you?"

Nodding, she whispered through those damaged lips, "Tell him he'll get a report in a week. Nothing else."

"You mean tell him nothing else? Or he'll get nothing else in a week?"

She blinked. "Tell nothing else. Keep the Victoria Sebastian CD and the computer to yourself. They are my only leverage."

"Last thing," I said, still speaking quietly.

Although her face was too swollen and bruised to show any expression, the intense stare of her eyes as she searched my face gave me a hint of her anxiety. I, too, hid my feelings. This was a woman I could love, but she had a boyfriend in California, so I would not permit myself to think of her as anything but a friend.

"Since I'm now your employee," I said, "exactly how much am I getting paid?"

I was rewarded by a slight upturn of her lips. Then the nurse shooed me away.

✛

As I left the hospital room, I thought about what I'd heard in my Jeep an hour earlier. The Victoria Sebastian CD.

In the last few months, I'd made an exception in an adulthood of relative frugality. With the windfall of my recent unexpected inheritance, I'd purchased a new Jeep TJ with a soft top. Black. Automatic, despite the fact that no right-thinking person, I believed, should drive an automatic Jeep. Why have an open-roof vehicle with crossbars, heavy suspension, and four-wheel drive and then neuter it with an automatic transmission? My previous Jeep had been a stick shift, and for years pride had been a strong enough motivator to overcome the pain and effort of driving with a prosthetic leg. Now, as much as it defied my beliefs about driving a Jeep, I'd finally begun to drive an automatic. I was grateful for the ease it offered me.

The new Jeep, unlike my previous one, also had the luxury of a compact disc player, with a six-disc changer hidden beneath the front seat. My tastes ran from classical to most of the pop music of the sixties and seventies, and I enjoyed the CD player almost as much as the automatic.

On the way to the hospital from Kellie's office, I had used the new player to listen to the Victoria Sebastian CD.

It did not contain music, but a brief phone call she'd recorded, then transferred to her laptop to burn it onto a compact disc. I'd found the disc, as she instructed, beneath the mousepad beside her computer.

The conversation had been short, and the voices belonged to Kellie and someone who had spoken quietly. I'd been forced to slow down and turn up the volume on my stereo and listen several times to hear the words clearly above the wind noise of the Jeep.

"Do you want to know why Victoria Sebastian disappeared?"

Then Kellie. "Who are you?"

"Remember the bodies. Under the lodge."

"How do you know this? Why are you telling me?"

"The bodies beneath the lodge. They hold the secret. That's all I can say."

"Can say? Or will say?"

"Find out what happened to Victoria Sebastian and you will have your answers. Good-bye."

I had no context in which to understand the message. Yet.

But I did know about the bodies police had discovered beneath a lodge dedicated to a local service organization, as did everyone else in Charleston. It had been the talk of the town in January. And I had my instructions.

Keep the recorded conversation away from Miles Ashby. Along with the files on Kellie's laptop.

✥

Ashby stood just down the hallway, massive arms crossed, smirking as a passing intern gave a concerned look at his holster and pistol.

"Give me all of it," he said. "Who Mixson has spoken to, what she's learned, if she thinks there's a case. I want transcripts and I want files. If she's going to be weeks or months in the hospital, I'm taking over."

"You need to understand something," I said. "Right now, I'm the only person in a position to give it to you. Kellie can't move out of that bed to get to the files and the interviews. Even if she knew where they were. I've already moved them somewhere safe."

I hoped the last part was accurate. I'd left the computer bag with Angel. Angel hadn't brought it into Kellie's room with the nurse, and Angel was smart enough to keep it safe when a guy like Ashby was asking Kellie questions.

"So?" Ashby asked.

If the computer was Kellie's only leverage, I hoped she'd forgive me for making it my only leverage against this man.

"So," I said, "if you want anything out of me, you'll go back in that hospital room and apologize to those two girls. Angel and Maddie. Address them by their names and apologize."

"Apologize?"

"What you called them was unacceptable." I'd spent years away from Charleston—in the dark time of my life when I was trying to run away from my past—and had lost much of its peculiar accent. But in times of stress, like now, it took hold of me as naturally as if I'd never been gone. "I expect your apology to be loud enough for Kellie and the nurse to hear exactly why you need to make it right for those two girls."

Ashby's face began to burn red.

"Sir," I said, "regardless of what Kellie directs me to do, I will trash those files and everything else pertinent to the case unless you tell those girls how wrong you were and give them your sincere apology."

It was my turn to wonder if he would take a swing at me. I shifted my weight to my good foot. Springing in any direction off a prosthesis is difficult, and I wanted to be ready.

"You'll pay for this," he finally grunted. And turned back to the hospital room.

That was my first indication of exactly how much those files might be worth.

CHAPTER

4

Roughly twenty-five years earlier, on a rainy April morning, two young Mormon men in white shirts and narrow black ties walked up the front steps of a large house that overlooked Colonial Lake on the Charleston Peninsula. They expected the massive front door, like all the others they'd knocked on vainly in the same neighborhood, to remain closed in silent censure of their serious-faced efforts.

Instead, it swung open on well-oiled hinges. Ever polite, they would have closed the door again and departed. But as one of the young men called a faintly hopeful greeting down the cavernous hallway, the other noticed something on the waxed hardwood just inside the door.

The splatters, not quite dried to a dull black, looked like blood.

Despite the best efforts of their parents, these young men had seen their share of television, especially detective shows. They knew that walking into a crime scene could destroy vital evidence. So they did what they felt would be scripted in such a situation. One remained on the front steps as the other hurried to a pay phone to call the police. Perhaps they expected that after a brief but expert forensic investigation and wisely placed questions to smug suspects, the possible crime would be as quickly solved as any one-hour television episode.

If so, they were about to learn how much real life differed from Hollywood's version.

The only similarity was in how the crime matched the excitement of any television show. The blood formed a trail through the main floor to the master bedroom and marked some of the bed's elegant silk sheets. The mirror above the chest of drawers had been smashed and various porcelain figurines shattered.

The blood type matched that of Victoria Sebastian, a twenty-five-year-old former Miss South Carolina who had caught the eye of John Sebastian, one of the pageant organizers, and married well enough to move into this neighborhood after a childhood of double-wide trailers. This blood match, however, had to be determined from hospital records, for there was no sign of Victoria Sebastian or her one-year-old daughter, Sophia.

Nor would there be in the years that followed.

Both had disappeared. Aside from the blood and evidence of a struggle in the bedroom, there were no other indications of their fate. Because there was no sign of forced entry at the front door or anywhere in the house, John Sebastian, five years older and at that time involved with a more recent beauty queen, was the main suspect. Yet without bodies, defense attorneys were able to argue that Victoria could have opened the door to anyone that morning, including the two young Mormons, who themselves had almost immediately faced a difficult interrogation unlike anything they'd witnessed on television.

John Sebastian was never charged with any crime. Among the more wealthy men living south of Broad, he cared little for what anyone thought of him. Six months after Victoria disappeared, beauty queen number two moved in with him as a common-law wife. To all appearances, they lived happily for the next decade, until queen number three, with the enticing name of Carmen, entered his life. Then John Sebastian endured an acrimonious separation and a hefty settlement to rid himself of queen number two.

By then Victoria had been legally declared dead. Carmen insisted on marriage. She also recognized John Sebastian's pattern and was smart enough to make him resign from his position as a pageant official. The Charleston aristocracy noted this event with glee, as well as how much less expensive it would have been for John Sebastian to follow the pattern closely enough to be an uncharged murder suspect with queen number two.

But queen number one had not been forgotten. All these years later, someone had anonymously hired a Chicago detective agency to search once more for the truth about Victoria Sebastian and her daughter. That agency, in turn, had contracted most of the work to the Charleston agency my friend Kellie Mixson had inherited from her father and ran on her own.

Nothing in her files showed that she had made much progress.

Except for the anonymous phone call directing her to the bodies beneath the lodge.

⊹

At eight o'clock in the evening after my visit to Kellie at the hospital, faint music reached me in my home office. Photocopies of the *Charleston Post and Courier* articles that told this story of John and Victoria Sebastian and his other two marriages covered my desk.

I stepped away from my computer and the report I'd been working on for Kellie. There was also a list of calls I needed to return on her behalf in the morning. In all, not much work to help a friend who needed it.

The faint music drew me. I moved to the window of my office that looked down on the house's inner courtyard, hidden from the street.

The center of the courtyard was made of ancient cobblestone taken from ballasts of the ships that used to carry slaves into Charleston's harbor. Moss showed green in the cracks of the stone, further softening its faded red. Wrought-iron lawn furniture and a stand-alone hammock were placed strategically to miss the midafternoon sun. Various vines and flowers crowded the edges of the courtyard and, during the day, drew hummingbirds and bees as if it were the original paradise.

Now, in the light of a full moon, the colors of the flowers had become a surrealistic monotone. Music played from outdoor speakers carefully hidden among the vines: The Righteous Brothers. "Unchained Melody."

Oh, my love, my darling, I hunger for your touch . . .

It was music that filled a soul with joyful melancholy, the yearning for an indefinable freedom that comes with hearing a distant train whistle in the night. Or watching an eagle soar, its pinion feathers separated and etched clearly against blue sky.

I wasn't the only one touched by the music and the moonlight or by the darkness of the shadows and the occasional flicker of a firefly. Angel and Maddie stood in the courtyard below, unaware that I was watching.

Maddie, only half Angel's height, leaned into her older sister, an arm wrapped around Angel's waist so that their figures seemed merged. They remained motionless, as fully captured by the moment as I was.

I wondered if Angel had chosen this music, started the stereo, and then stepped outside with Maddie, fully understanding the song's power. I wondered if Angel was speaking quietly to Maddie about the mother they had lost, telling Maddie about the birthday parties and Christmas mornings and trips to the zoo that Angel remembered. Or if Angel was telling Maddie about their Grammie Zora and how fiercely the old woman had protected them. Or if Angel was sharing dreams and hopes—all they might become and all that waited for them in the world as they grew older.

Their tenderness touched me; I would have been a robot if it had not. But what surprised me was the depth of my protective love for both of them. Was this what parents felt for their children? Or was a parent's love far deeper than I would ever understand, my love merely a shadow of the real thing? I was just their guardian, not a man who had watched their births, held them, and rocked them to sleep as infants. Even more, if a parent's love could be that much deeper than mine, how much more were we loved by God? My life since returning to Charleston had taught me a great deal about God's love, real love, and I'd come to know more of what I'd missed as my faith deepened.

The music itself was poetry.

I understood, even as I watched them, how fragile and precious this moment was, like the dust of a butterfly's wing. I tried to breathe in this memory, wanting to be able to summon it someday in the winter of my life.

The moment ended with the song and with Angel's movement. She pulled herself away from Maddie and faced her, taking both her little hands.

A new song reached me through my closed office window. Upbeat, vigorous, and joyful, with no trace of melancholy. Angel threw her head back, and her teeth gleamed briefly in the moonlight as she laughed.

She began to dance, still holding one of Maddie's hands. And Maddie danced with her, throwing her other little fist in the air as she pumped her arms. There was no structure to their dance, just the delighted spontaneous movements that only children enjoy with no trace of self-consciousness.

I watched them dance until the song ended, until Angel pulled Maddie close and hugged her. Then they walked inside, and all that remained was my memory. Almost as if I'd witnessed a shooting star and could only wonder if it had really flashed by in its brief glory.

CHAPTER

5

Months earlier, after Angel and Maddie and I had moved into the mansion, during an unusually cold spell, a water pipe had burst at the Freemason lodge in one of the old boroughs of Charleston. Repair work the next morning, the second of January, had led workmen to seven caskets hidden in a crawl space beneath the floor.

Although the caskets held the hair and skulls and bones of seven men, I can say with confidence that few of the aristocrats I grew up around would have expressed much more than bored cynicism when the subject came up during their rounds of regular cocktail parties over the following weekends. For one thing, at the parties south of Broad Street, bored cynicism and amused irony were as de rigueur as the proper knot on the proper tie, a meaningless adornment unless the wearer bore the equally proper combination of first and last names.

For another, these people were recipients of wealth built by ancestors whose ranks included crooked politicians, plantation owners, slave traders, pirates, rumrunners, and assorted Civil War profiteers. Since it was expected that every aristocratic family in Charleston had its share of skeletons in the closet, there was no need to bother with much commotion at yet another scandal, even if this one was a literal exposure of long-hidden bones.

Lastly, for decades upon decades there had been rumors of a secret society that guided Charlestonian politics and power and banking and law. These rumors were something for the aristocracy of each new generation to shrug off with hidden pride—a shrug that implied they were above caring, above suspicion, and most naturally of all, above any laws that applied to lesser Charlestonians. In other words, if this society existed, it existed because they not only allowed it, but sanctioned it. And how delicious the irony that the person raising weary eyebrows at the rumor might actually belong to this secret society.

Local and national media fervor died within a week of the discovery; right-wing AM radio hosts stopped ranting about Freemason conspiracies within two weeks. Soon enough the seven caskets were forgotten by most, except for the guides of Charleston walking tours, who had immediately begun to detour their gaggles of elderly ladies past the Freemason lodge, delighting the blue-rinsed out-of-towners with lurid speculation about the reasons and causes of the deaths of the seven men.

Among the few to give the matter more than passing

attention were detectives of the Charleston Police Department. As required, they continued to work quietly to identify the seven men and discover how they had died.

In March, public interest flared briefly when one pile of bones was publicly identified as the earthly remains of Whitman Metiere, a sixth-generation Charlestonian who had proudly claimed he was from an unholy eighteenth-century marriage between a pirate and brothel madam accused but not convicted of poisoning her first husband, a man of great wealth but obviously limited judgment in women.

This lack of morality seemed genetic. During his adult years among the elite, from the 1920s until he vanished from society in 1958, Whitman Metiere excelled in cutthroat business as much as he did in decadence. He was able to build a relatively large inheritance into a monstrous one. Buried in the foundation of his expanding empire were the carcasses of lesser businesses he'd destroyed by various unscrupulous methods.

Because Whitman Metiere disappeared several years before I was born, my knowledge of his life is limited to gossip I absorbed growing up in a waterfront mansion barely three blocks from the Metiere home. During my childhood, it was commonly believed that Whitman Metiere had chosen to take advantage of money hidden in Zurich accounts and flee American soil because of a scandal that involved his weakness for teenage girls.

The last anyone remembered seeing Metiere's face was the afternoon of October 31, a yearly date remarkable to his family because of the Metiere tradition of throwing its famed masquerade ball on the evening before All Saints' Day. The tradition began during Charleston's plantation days, and it was a well-established peculiarity of the Metieres from that era forward to require that none of the partygoers give the evening its more common name, Halloween. It was, as the Metiere hosts of each generation insisted, All Hallows' Eve. The Metieres took pride in all their traditions and pointed out that the traditional mass on All Saints' Day had once been called *Allhallowmas*. Ever good Anglicans, the Metieres generally supported the rites of their religion and, in particular, the honor this one bestowed upon Christian saints, grateful that merely going through rites was a much easier task than following the spirit behind them.

Although Whitman Metiere was seen that afternoon, hurrying down King Street from one shop to another with last-minute preparations for the gala event, no one remembers him at his own party that evening. This in itself was not peculiar. No one could identify anyone with much certainty on that occasion.

The Metiere masquerade ball was and is notorious for two things: excess in fashionable mind-altering substances and the single, strictly enforced rule that all attendees must be costumed and remain in complete masquerade the entire evening. Those two factors made the party famous and the invitations coveted.

The blend of inebriated senses and anonymity of a hundred or so people against a background of loud music, shrieks, and laughter allowed the attending Charlestonians one evening to break free of the public roles they were forced to play all the other days of the year. As to be expected in such a situation, many of the excesses were outrageous. But this only added to the mystique of the annual party.

The excuses and denials and embellished stories that were whispered in the days after each masquerade became known—always with a wink and a grin at the amusing paradox—as the lies of saints.

With the discovery of the bones and hair of Whitman Metiere in one of the caskets beneath the Freemason lodge, it became obvious in retrospect that on the night of October 31, 1958, perhaps murder had joined the host of sins concealed by those lies of the saints.

And now—if the cryptic message delivered to Kellie could be believed—those sins might also explain the disappearance or murder of a former beauty queen and her young daughter.

✛

"I've got a bad feeling about this," Jubil Smith said, ignoring the photocopies of news stories about Victoria Sebastian I'd laid before him. "You don't offer to buy me breakfast just to show me that you know how to go through newspaper archives like any tenth grader on a school report."

"That's why I came to you," I said. "I needed someone smart enough to see through me like that."

"Or maybe I'm the only person you know on the force."

I handed him a folded piece of paper with my handwriting in pencil on the inside. "Short shopping list," I said, "since you're the only person I know on the force."

Jubil glared at me. It was an effective glare. He was coal black, an elegantly threatening man with an athlete's build, muscle that he carried well although he was past his football career. We'd played high school football together—he was quarterback and I was receiver—before the car accident that had forced the removal of my right leg below the knee. He'd gone on to a brief stint in pro ball and was now a detective with the Charleston police. His glare would have intimidated most people. But I'd known him far too long and simply returned his stare with a bland smile.

Our waitress stopped at the table and refilled our coffees. We were at the Sweetwater Café on Tradd Street. It was a place where the locals came early. The tourists came later, seeking the authenticity of a diner that served grits and pancakes and waffles, along with a laid-back attitude.

"No thanks," Jubil said, handing me back the list without looking at it. "Don't even have my own shopping list. Because I don't do groceries. Hardly ever for my wife and never for other people."

I set the paper down between us and smiled again. I wasn't going to let him say no to this one. "Say you had a friend who was in the hospital and couldn't get the groceries for herself," I said. "Say you were the only person she could ask. Say this was a person who had done you favors over the years, like getting information from the streets you'd have a tough time getting yourself. Say this person really needed help and you were the only person who could give it."

Jubil groaned and muttered under his breath. He knew I was talking about Kellie. Jubil had been the one to call me to the hospital while she was in her first surgery. He had paced around with me in the waiting room the entire six hours it took to hear she would at least make it through the night.

"It's not a big deal," I said. "Really. Some Chicago agency contracted her to look into the Victoria Sebastian disappearance. She asked me to wrap up her report, and she needs a few loose ends tucked into place. I get the feeling if she doesn't finish the job, she won't get paid. And right now, she probably needs income more than she wants us to know. I doubt she's got a great insurance plan for medical or disability. I don't know about you, but when friends need help . . ."

Jubil groaned again. "That's low, Nick." He picked up the paper and unfolded it.

The list consisted of only two things. All I wanted was a copy of the police report on the original investigation and a meeting with the detective who'd been in charge.

Jubil's shoulders relaxed. "This is it?"

I carefully avoided Jubil's question. "Kellie asked me to meet with Victoria Sebastian's former physician and ask a few questions. That should wrap most of it up. She's already done most of what she felt needed doing. My real job is to put together a report for her from all the interviews she did. I finished that last night."

Despite his justified suspicion of my invitation to breakfast, Jubil's professional curiosity took over. "Did Kellie learn anything?"

I thought of the phone call she'd recorded. *The bodies beneath the lodge. They hold the secret. That's all I can say. . . . Find out what happened to Victoria Sebastian and you will have your answers.* "I'm guessing if she found anything important, she'd want to talk to you directly," I said.

"So it's a one-way street. You get what you want from me but give nothing in return."

"Not me. Kellie. Remember? I merely represent her."

Jubil grunted. "You said this came down from a Chicago agency?"

"Kellie tells me it's normal. Subcontracting local agencies. Kellie's got a lot more sources in Charleston than they do." I grinned. "Sources like you."

"Humph. Any idea who hired the Chicago agency? Strange that someone wants this checked out after all this time."

I shook my head.

"You don't know who hired the Chicago agency, or Kellie doesn't know?"

"Both," I answered.

"Interesting." Jubil took a drink of coffee and grimaced. He always complained about too much caffeine in his diet. He'd never cut back as far as I could ever see. "If this were my case, I'd make it a point to know who was behind it. That would tell me a lot."

"So make it your case. Unofficially."

"Not a chance." Jubil handed me the list again. "Got enough on my plate with cases that belong to this decade."

"Funny."

"You should appreciate me more for that."

"I'd appreciate you getting me the things on that list."

"Just this once," Jubil said.

"Thanks."

"For a smart cop like me, no problem." He gave me a tight smile. "But you're the one with a problem. See, I already knew you were involved in this. Probably the only reason I made it seem like I was getting suckered into this breakfast meeting."

I added some cream to my coffee. And waited.

"Miles Ashby," Jubil said. "Know him?"

"Chicago detective agency," I said, impressed that Jubil was already that far ahead of me.

"He's an engine about to blow a gasket," Jubil said. "He stopped by the station about six last evening. Wanted some kid busted."

I did my math. Six last evening. That was shortly after he'd left the hospital. "Angel?"

"The fact you can make that guess so accurately bothers me, Nick. We both know you're under some scrutiny here. If Angel can't stay out of trouble . . ."

He didn't add the rest. Angel had a history of bending the law to take care of Maddie. In fact, she'd thrown a stolen cell phone in my lap the first day we met. Jubil and I both knew why Angel and Maddie were on their own and in need of a guardian. Jubil had risked his career to keep her out of the system. I was a temporary guardian only because Jubil had pulled strings to arrange it. I still needed to go through bureaucratic hoops to become their permanent guardian.

"Tell me about last night," I said quietly.

"The boys at the station know that you and Angel are on my radar. When Ashby came in to file a complaint about her, I got a quick call. They held him in the waiting room until I made it to the station. He lays into me like I'm the one who stole his wallet."

"Wallet." A quick picture of the hospital room flashed through my mind. Of Ashby's suit jacket on the chair by Kellie's bed, unguarded while he and I stepped into the hallway.

"Wallet. So today I'm supposed to do an official police interview with the person he's accused of taking it. Grace Louise Starr, aka Angel."

"Let me ask her about it first, all right? And in Angel's defense—"

"You saying she did it?"

"I'm saying he said something no kid should have to hear."

"What's that?"

"When you get a chance," I said, "ask Ashby yourself. I'll be curious to know how he answers."

Jubil studied my face. Must have seen the controlled anger. Sighed. "Get back to me on the wallet," he said. "Sooner instead of later."

C H A P T E R

6

Osier's Medical Supplies was squeezed between a tattoo parlor
and a pawnshop. Its street-front sign was hand painted, and the
grime on the once-white stucco matched the ancient grime
that leached color from all the other narrow buildings on the
street.

I'd driven here with legitimate preconceptions. I knew
the neighborhood from the address in Kellie's file. It was
located well north of Broad, in an area known for drug addicts
and prostitutes.

I parked illegally in front of the building for three reasons.
First, it was raining. Second, the shorter distance I walked, the
less chance a junkie might decide I was worthwhile prey. The
last reason was the obvious gleaming newness of my Jeep.
Although the rain had forced me to put up the top before leav-

ing for this area, it still offered little protection against a determined thief. I knew this area had more than a few.

I hurried across the street, not even certain the door to Osier's Medical Supplies would be open. I'd made three calls from my cell phone on the drive here, and only the bored female voice on an answering machine had responded each time, promising that business hours were nine to five on weekdays. It was ten till eleven on a Monday morning; why, then, had no one answered?

A sign on the door said Closed. I tried to squint inside, but the blacked-out windows served their purpose.

Then the door opened, slowly enough that I had time to move back. A thin young woman with badly bleached hair stepped outside, holding a baby wrapped in a blanket. When she gave me a wan smile, I saw teeth darkened by decay.

"Doctor Osier inside?" I asked.

"You don't want to see him," she said quickly.

"No?"

"You look like you can afford better than Doc O." Evidently she'd taken in my golf shirt, khaki pants, and fresh haircut and decided I didn't belong in this neighborhood. She kissed her little girl on the forehead. "Come on, Chantelle. Let's get you home."

I nearly let her walk away. That would have been easier. After all, it was pretty clear to me what profession the woman was in. In the past, I would have—and not even thought about it later. But having Angel and Maddie in my life had made me start thinking more about other people. People like this woman, a mother with her child.

"Hey," I said.

She turned back to me, her face reflecting both hope that I might become a customer and disappointment for the same reason.

"Let me give you a number," I said, "in case you ever want out of the life."

Her face instantly twisted into anger and suspicion. "My life's my business, pal. Maybe I like it the way it is."

"Let me ask you something," I said softly. "Is it something you'd want for Chantelle?"

She blinked a few times.

"Whatever you want for her," I said, "is something you deserve too."

I heard a quick intake of breath.

I pulled a twenty from my wallet and wrote down the phone number for Mount Carmel African Methodist Episcopal Church. "Call anytime," I said, holding out the bill. "Ask for Pastor Samuel Thorpe, and tell him you got the number from Nick. That's me. What's your name?"

She took the twenty grudgingly. "Cyndi. With a y, then an i."

"Cyndi," I repeated.

She clutched Chantelle tightly. "In answer to your question, Doc O.'s inside. He's always inside; that man ain't missed a day in five years, and he won't take a dime. Just don't get on his wrong side."

"Wrong side?"

"Government people don't understand why he does what he does. Keep looking to regulate and license him and make sure he ain't a front for drugs, which he ain't. You don't look like government, but you also don't look like the kind that needs him. All I'm saying is . . ." She shrugged. "Well, if you want to find out, just open that door."

About the same time I was opening Osier's door, another meeting was about to take place at Charleston International Airport, near one of the gates for United Airlines.

Miles Ashby, the same man who had stood threateningly over Kellie's hospital bed, stood near the pay phone farthest down the wall, his back to the tall windows that overlooked the runway. Here his corporate attire served him well. Unless one scrutinized the mass of his shoulders beneath his suit jacket, he resembled just another road warrior with glazed eyes and sore feet. But he watched every new arrival to the gate area closely, hiding his curiosity behind a veil of feigned disinterest.

He had decided that whoever had arranged the meeting would be a man, so he gave them the most attention. Over several minutes, three different men approached him, then veered off. A middle-aged pseudojock in an Adidas sweat suit. A sullen Harley-Davidson longhair. A corporate type in a fake Armani with a cell phone to his ear. Any one of them, Ashby thought with a quickening of adrenaline, could be the guy.

So Ashby was fooled by the bent old man with a red-veined nose and the incongruous combination of John Deere cap, worn herringbone suit jacket, lavender dress shirt, and shiny brown corduroys. The old man hobbled closer with the help of a gnarled wooden cane and mumbled an apology as he squeezed past Ashby. He made his way to the window and stood there, gazing at the baggage handlers below.

My first glimpse of Dr. Leonard Osier came after fifteen minutes in the small front room. Unlike the grim exterior, this room was brightly painted with murals of zoo animals. A children's play area occupied the center of the room. Soft muted light from wall sconces fell across the leather couches that lined the walls. The aroma of fresh coffee wafted from a pot on a stand in the corner.

Despite the fact that four mothers, each with a couple of children, were on the couches, it wasn't overly noisy. Two of the children, obviously not feeling well, silently clung to their mothers. The other children played happily at their mothers' feet, while the women engaged in pleasant chitchat. Two old men sat on stools in the far corner, sipping coffee and watching the children.

None of these people was well dressed. It was obvious from their clothing and hair and body odor that they lived in this part of town. I was the one who was out of place, but I did not receive hostile stares.

Except from Dr. Osier.

My first glimpse was of a man wearing a stethoscope, a clinical white jacket, and blue jeans. As an old woman in an overcoat stepped into the room through a door that led from the back part of the narrow building, he followed her and patted her shoulder. She thanked him for his time. His wrinkles, gray hair, round glasses, and wide face gave him an aura of friendly authority. He looked at least seventy but held himself with the posture of a man twenty years younger.

He glanced at me once with fierce suspicion, then ignored me. "Brandi?" he called.

One of the children, a six-year-old girl burrowed against her mother's side, looked up from her sanctuary on the couch. Osier smiled kindly at her, a complete contrast to the stern distrust he had directed my way.

Brandi's mother stood and took the girl's hand. "Time for the nice doctor to make you better."

Osier held the door open for them. I briefly glimpsed a hallway with more zoo murals. The doctor followed mother and daughter, and the door shut on the rest of us.

I leaned back and waited again, my curiosity about this enigmatic doctor growing.

"Be nice," the old man at the window said to Miles Ashby in a conversational tone, "to someday fly first class. That would take money, though. Plenty of it."

Ashby told me later that he ignored the old man at first.

"You like money?" the old man asked. " 'Course you do. That suit—"

"Shut it," Miles said, with as little rancor as if he'd swatted at a fly. He kept his stare forward, determined to spot the man he was waiting for on his approach.

"See what money does?" the old man said. "Gets you a suit that makes you look surface good. Hides what's inside, just waiting to bust out of that expensive fabric and those hand-sewn stitches. The foster homes, time on the streets. All that hard, mean time just boiling inside, ready to blow."

Slowly, like a lion scenting its prey, Miles turned his head toward the old man. "You?" Miles asked.

"That stuff about boiling inside I got that from your therapy records," the old man said. "What I don't know about you ain't worth knowing. Make this a lesson. Don't under-estimate me."

"Not much left to underestimate if I kill you."

The old man shook his head. "That's the reason I sent those United tickets with the note. Gets us to this side of the metal detectors. Means I'm clean. Means you're clean. Tell me you didn't think about that while you were waiting, wishing you had your fancy pistol your permit lets you carry. Waiting and wondering who set this up."

"I thought about it. And about how much I hate games. Now I'm thinking how I could snap your neck like a chicken bone. It'd make a nice little noise—*pop*—and the only person would hear it is me."

"This time of day too many people around for you to do any bone snapping. Believe me, I haven't found a better place to meet, and I've been doing this awhile."

"I got other things on the go," Miles said. "This better be worth it."

The old man shrugged, his bony shoulders sliding around inside the too-big suit jacket. "It's my money on your tickets. In the old days, you didn't need tickets and ID to get past security. Wish Southwest flew into Charleston. Round-trip tickets sometimes as cheap as Greyhound bus. At least I picked up a ticket to somewhere nice. Three hours from now, I'll be in Miami, whether or not you like what I got to say. Your tickets to D.C.? Use 'em or don't. Matters nothing to me. I'm happy knowing you can't follow me to Miami. But now we're in a place where we can talk. Safe."

The old man pointed his cane at a Starbucks stand near the next gate. "There's an hour before my flight leaves. For us to talk, I gotta sit down. My legs are killing me. I covered the tickets. What's fair is you buy the coffee."

"Not a chance, old man. I'm done with this unless you give me one good reason to stick around."

"Didn't you hear me before? What I don't know about you ain't worth knowing."

"Good-bye, old man."

"Victoria Sebastian and that detective broad. You've been paid to duplicate those reports before you send them back to Chicago. You want me to tell you how much, when, and where the payments reached you, and how stupid you've been with the money? Say I call the IRS and tell them about the accounts with all those cash deposits. Stupid, stupid, stupid. Don't you know anything about hiding your tracks?"

"Someday, I get the chance, you're dead."

As he moved to a nearby seat, the old man grinned widely, showing surprisingly good white teeth. "I take cream in my coffee. Make it a big one. And get me one of those fancy biscuits that you got to soak in the coffee to make it soft enough to chew. I'll be here when you get back."

As I waited in Dr. Osier's office, other patients arrived from the street at irregular intervals. A sullen teenager. An obese middle-aged woman who walked with a cane. A heavily pregnant woman with a toddler in a stroller. It was a two-way turnstile, however, because every five or ten minutes Dr. Osier would invite someone to the back part of the building as another left, smiling and thanking him.

It didn't take me long to realize that, for all practical purposes, the front part of Osier's Medical Supplies was a waiting room, similar in many ways to one at a private clinic. This one, however, had no receptionist. No computer for patient records. And, as far as I could tell, no system for billing. I wondered if all that was somewhere in the back, where Dr. Osier led his patients. I doubted it. Practicality dictated that the best place to treat patients as a number was the funnel point, where I sat.

Waiting.

Osier came and went half a dozen times, each time glaring at me, then smiling at his next patient. Later, he simply ignored me.

I found it both irritating and amusing and decided early that I would not let him win at his little game. Besides, he'd equipped the room with plenty of back issues of *Reader's Digest*, and the coffee, if my guess was right, came from freshly ground Starbucks beans. There were worse places to wait.

Three hours and seven *Reader's Digests* later, the front room was empty of patients except for me. Dr. Osier said good-bye to his final patient, an old woman, from the doorway and shut the door again.

It only made me more determined to wait.

A few minutes later the door opened and Osier peeked out. He winced when he saw that I was still there. "If you're here for free medical advice, I doubt you qualify." He had a gravelly voice, the kind that belonged to doctors who spent a lifetime smoking against the advice they doled out to their patients.

"No and yes."

His frown became puzzled.

"No, I'm not here for medical advice," I said. "And yes, I don't qualify."

"Good-bye then," he said and began to close the door.

"Victoria Sebastian," I said, "and her daughter. Someone wants them found."

The door opened slowly. He moved completely out into the waiting room. "You get fifteen minutes of my time. At the fee I used to charge my other patients. The ones south of Broad."

"You'll take a check?"

He smiled. His first one in my direction. "With two pieces of ID."

✣

At the airport, the old man in the John Deere hat was leaning forward—one hand holding a fresh cup of coffee, the other dipping a scone—and speaking as if Miles Ashby were a schoolboy.

"Forty years back, maybe longer, I started doing what I do. Facilitating. Somebody on one side needs something done; I find the person on the other side to do it. It's dirty stuff, mostly, that I arrange. The less everyone on both sides knows the better. Most of the time, I arrange it through letters, phone calls, drop-offs. Except today, I'm here in person."

Ashby was angry but curious enough to restrain himself. He listened, checking around occasionally to make sure nobody sat within hearing distance of their conversation.

"Forty years." The old man pulled the scone from his coffee and sucked on it before chewing off a bite. "Job like mine doesn't come with a pension."

He was a sloppy eater, speaking as he chewed, and Ashby looked away.

"I'm not in a position to make my employer pay for my retirement," the old man continued. "But I'd like to get there. And that's how you can make some serious money. With me. What you've been getting for those reports is nothing." He paused to look directly at Ashby. "I know you're interested, boy," the old man said. "What I'm trying to decide is how and when you're going to try and step over me to pull the fruit off the tree. So listen good. It'll be the last thing you do."

"Who's your employer?"

"If I knew," the old man said, "I wouldn't be here having this conversation with an animal like you."

"Forty years and you don't know."

The old man slurped his coffee. "Forty years and I don't know. Neither did my old man. Near as I could tell, he'd worked for the same employer just as long. Got old, decided to pass on the work to me. He helped me with it as long as he could. Day he died, he was at the Catholic church, giving somebody instructions in the confessional booth. If I had a boy of my own, I'd pass on the job myself. It's been good to our family. Been a good thing to inherit."

"I've had enough," Ashby said. "Jerk someone else around with your mumbo jumbo."

"Get me a big enough lever and I can move the world."

"Huh?"

"Some Greek said that. Or something like it. He's been dead a long time. But it don't change the truth of it. Find the right lever, and you can get what you want."

"Anyone ever tell you that you talk like a dog chasing its tail?"

"I facilitate. But to facilitate, you have to know how to lever someone. Money, revenge, fear—there's always something. For you, it's money. I already know that. My employer? After all these years, I've got the lever it takes. Blackmail. I just don't know where to put that lever."

"All right then," Ashby said. Grudgingly. "What do you think that lever is worth?"

The old man gave him a number.

Ashby whistled. And lost a lot of his hostility. "You, old man," Ashby said, "could be good for my soul."

"Nicholas Barrett."

I nodded. Osier handed back my driver's license.

"Lift your pant leg. The side you favored with your limp."

We had moved back to a well-equipped medical office with an examining table. I sat in one chair. He sat in another, facing me.

I did as he asked.

"Higher. And roll down your sock."

Again, I did as requested.

He nodded at the sight of my prosthesis. "You're the one. Nearly got killed in a drunk-driving car accident. Ran away. You were what, twenty at the time?"

"Nineteen. The *Post and Courier* ran that follow-up story nearly a year ago, right after I returned to Charleston," I said. "I'm impressed you remember."

"Don't read newspapers. Or watch the news. Remembered the intern who took your leg off. And, as a wing of the hospital is named after your family, it's something a person tends not to forget."

He steepled his fingers beneath his chin. "So you've returned to Charleston. Don't bother telling me the details. You're down to twelve minutes, and I have no doubt there are already more patients waiting."

"You don't charge them."

"That's my business . . . and God's. But back to Victoria Sebastian. You said someone wants Victoria and her daughter found. I presume you mean their bodies."

"I'm making no guesses either way. I'm here on behalf of a client who wants to know more about her disappearance."

"Now you've got to show me other identification. Police. Private eye. Whatever gives you the right to do this."

"Don't have it," I said. "Didn't know that was required once I paid the outrageous doctor's fee for fifteen minutes of your time."

Osier grunted. "Fair enough. Victoria Sebastian. What do you want to know?"

"She was a patient of yours. One from south of Broad."

"Perhaps. I had a forty-year career as general practitioner. That's a lot of patients to juggle in my memory."

"Strange," I said with a smirk. "You remember my case, and I wasn't even your patient. John Sebastian inherited one of the biggest trust funds in Charleston. His wife Victoria was the apparent victim in a high-profile police case for at least six months until they gave up the search. And you don't remember that?"

"Touché. I will not tell you anything that violates doctor-patient privilege. Nor will I be unintelligent enough to say anything about her medical record that would lead John Sebastian to sue me for slander. He's an extremely wealthy man, after all."

"I see," I said, wondering if I did. Was the doctor trying to tell me something?

"There's an old joke," Osier said. "The one where you ask someone if he's stopped beating his wife. It's only funny, of course, because any answer the person can give sounds incriminating. I've often wondered if John Sebastian would find it amusing. If you have a chance someday, ask him." Then Osier met my eyes directly. "Then ask him the same joke again, but exchange the word *wife* for *children*. I believe what the Bible says about Judgment Day. Some people will get what they deserve, and some will receive better. But it won't change what's happened."

Osier stood. "Your fifteen minutes is not up, but I think we're finished here."

"Certainly."

He took my arm and escorted me to the hallway. Surprisingly, he didn't let go. "If a person had hospital connections, that person might try to find out how many times Victoria Sebastian had been admitted with various injuries the first two years of her marriage to John Sebastian."

His grip on my elbow tightened. "A person might also check the medical records of their son and daughter."

"Son?" I asked. "I thought she only had a daughter."

Osier released my arm. "Good-bye, Mr. Barrett. And God bless you in your search. I would be curious someday to find out where your questions take you."

✜

"Let me get this straight," Ashby said to the old man. He'd listened another ten minutes to him. Like a schoolboy. "I find out who hired the Chicago agency. We use that to link what we've got about Victoria Sebastian to your employer."

The old man nodded. A drop of coffee remained at the end of his nose from when he'd tilted the coffee cup back as far as possible. "Unless you already know who hired the agency."

Ashby shook his head. "Won't tell."

"Because you don't know?"

"Not even going to give you that."

"Six weeks of passing on the detective broad's work, and now you get scruples."

"I'm in, old man; don't worry about that. I'm just not giving you anything until I know I'm going to get what you promised me. Facilitator like you probably knows a lot of ways to cut me out."

"I do. But I won't."

"Two things. First one is, what's your name?"

"Jones." He grinned. "And don't try to find out different."

"Fair enough. Second thing. Why? Forty years of milking the same cow. Why try to kill it now?"

"Something's changed. The detective broad learned something. Something that's made my employer worried enough to want her dead. Only I can't figure what it is just yet. Need more."

"What do you mean, want her dead?"

"I'm a facilitator." Jones grinned again. "You really think that truck hitting her was an accident?"

C H A P T E R

7

"We're late," Angel announced more cheerfully than I would have preferred. We had just arrived at the antique shop. Angel had called the housekeeper to confirm that Maddie was doing fine without her. "Nick's Jeep got towed. It's still in the impound. It was his fault. Good thing he called or I would have been worried."

"That's nice, dear," Glennifer Beloise replied. She'd been waiting at the door for us. She lifted her bony wrist and pulled back the sleeve of her dress to examine her watch. "Hurry now. Did you remember what I requested?"

"In my backpack," Angel said. "Printed it off the Internet."

Glennifer took her by the hand and led her away.

Something was wrong. I could smell it. I knew Glennifer and her spinster twin, Elaine, very well. After all, my mother had brought me to this shop when I was a boy. The two ladies were institutions in the antique business and in Charleston, and I had counted on their knowledge over the last year: the disappearance of my mother and the reappearance of a price-less work of art.

As I thought about Glennifer's welcome, my suspicion grew. For one thing, she had been waiting at the front of the shop instead of in her usual spot—in the office at the back with Elaine. For another, Glennifer's friendliness to Angel and Angel's friendliness in return were unusual, to say the least. They hadn't gotten off on a good foot from the very beginning of their relationship. And the lack of reaction to Angel's report about the Jeep was my third reason for suspicion.

For Glennifer and Elaine, anything out of the ordinary routine demanded immediate knowledge of all the facts, dissection of the decisions made by all parties involved, and strong opinions on the correctness or incorrectness of those decisions. While this love of gossip was a business asset—it was said that whenever Glennifer or Elaine visited a blue blood's house to purchase furniture, it was a sure sign of an impending foreclosure—these endless discussions were an eccentricity of their personal lives as well.

Not that my Jeep being towed during the hours I'd been in Osier's waiting room was a major news event. For me, it had simply been an irritating inconvenience; I'd emerged from Osier's cheerful waiting room to find my parking place empty. During my cab ride to Angel's school, I'd left a voice mail on Angel's cell so she wouldn't worry about my lateness in picking her up for our daily visit to the antique shop.

To Glennifer and Elaine, however, my carelessness leading to an impounded vehicle was fodder for at least an hour's
worth of conversation. They knew everything about everyone,
and they were always adding to their storehouse of information. Their knowledge had certainly proved important to me.

Is it someone's birthday? As I stood in the entranceway of
the antique shop with the door half open, I tried to decide
what event I'd forgotten and whether I needed to worry. By
then, Glennifer and Angel had navigated the maze of antique
furniture to the back office. That too was alarming. Of late,
Angel had spent most of her time among the antiques and was
currently trying to convince Glennifer to lower the price on a
Queen Anne square stool.

"Willy?"

"For heaven's sakes," he said. "Shut the door. I can feel a
cold coming on as it is, and the damp air is a terror on my
sinuses."

He was standing on a chair beside an armoire, armed with
a feather duster, pretending to work. Willy was almost as much
of a fixture as the ancient fluorescent lights. He was short, with
a thin mustache on a squirrel-thin face and his dark hair slicked
back. I'd never seen him without a bow tie beneath his suit
jacket. His effeminate air hid a toughness that I suspected but
hadn't seen tested.

I shook my umbrella clear of rain, then brought it inside
and closed the door. "Willy? Anything happening?"

"As a matter of fact, yes," he said. "In the last minute, my
heart has beaten another eighty or ninety times closer to the
moment it will finally stop. To think, all I've been able to do

with that time is wait with anticipation for the moment I'm alone with this oh-so-precious furniture again."

At least Willy was behaving normally.

"Ah . . . ah . . . ," I said as I walked by. I stopped and drew some deep breaths as if I were about to sneeze.

Willy whipped a red handkerchief from his pocket and covered his face.

"False alarm," I said. "So sorry."

I smiled and moved on. My victories were so few in this shop that I had to enjoy them while I could.

I found Glennifer and Elaine and Angel already seated. Pot of tea already brewed. Glennifer and Elaine stared at the telephone atop the papers scattered on the desk they shared.

"Hello," I said. At least there was no birthday cake with lit candles.

They ignored me, gazing at the phone like two cats with a wounded mouse at their feet. Each wore a black dress on her slender frame. They moved almost identically, shaped their silver hair identically, and apparently thought identically. They were fond of finishing each other's sentences.

"Hello?" I repeated. Louder.

"Shhh," Glennifer said. She glanced at her watch. The phone rang and Glennifer smiled at Elaine. Elaine nodded. Then she frantically searched the desk for her reading glasses, which she handed to Glennifer. Glennifer nodded thanks, slipped on the glasses, and picked up a sheet of paper.

Clearing her throat, she answered the phone. "This is Glennifer Beloise," she said, her eyes on the sheet of paper. "How may I help?"

✦

Kellie told me later that she received two visitors that day. I would learn about them during my evening visit, when I reported what I'd learned from Dr. Leonard Osier.

Kellie's first visitor was a former beauty queen.

"I read in the papers what happened to you," Carmen Sebastian said. "Then I had to wait until John went on a business trip before I could come to visit."

Carmen sat beside Kellie's bed. Her skin had the tawny glow of a woman who worked out regularly. The expensive clothing matched the air of someone who had once walked pageant stages to the winner's circle.

"I'm here because I need help." Carmen spoke in a hushed, little-girl voice, as if she were still a ten-year-old competing in junior pageants. "It might not be easy to believe what I'm going to tell you."

Kellie motioned at a glass of water and a straw.

"No thanks," Carmen said.

Kellie pointed at herself.

"Oh." Carmen gave her the glass.

"Thanks." Kellie tilted her head to sip the water as she listened.

"The one bad thing I might have to say about my husband is that his temper is horrible," Carmen began. "He's so sweet afterward that it almost makes it worthwhile. I know that sounds crazy, maybe. But fighting and then making up—well, at least it's more exciting than never talking to each other. I got some friends, that's what they tell me it's like to be married to their husbands. As long as he doesn't get crazy anymore, I can handle one or two punches, especially if it means he leaves the kids alone. Yeah, I can see on your face that you feel bad for me. Thanks."

Carmen patted Kellie's hand. "But it's not as bad as before, and I don't want to leave him. He's so good to us the rest of the time. And there's been no more trips to the hospital for me or the kids. Ever since the day something came in the mail for him. That's what I wanted to tell you about.

"Normally, if something is addressed to him, I leave it alone. I don't want to know about his monthly bill from the country club, stuff like that. But this letter, it had his name on it in hand-writing. Block letters. You maybe know about my husband's history. Used to like dating new girls while he was still married. I know he's a lot older now and not as energetic as he used to be, but I wasn't stupid. I made him quit his involvement with the Miss South Carolina event. I mean, he was a great catch, and I have no regrets about where I live now. But why risk losing him to someone else younger? So I opened the letter. Steamed it open like you see in the movies. Works okay. There was nothing inside except a folded piece of paper with a drawing on it. What I did was go into his home office and run it through his fax machine so I had a copy of it. Just because it seemed weird that the letter has no return address and all it has in it is this cross-shaped drawing. Then I resealed the envelope with the original paper in it and let him open it that night when he got home."

Kellie put up her hands to stop Carmen. "Cross-shaped."

Carmen nodded. "That's what I said. Cross-shaped. Like from a medieval history book. And that night, when he opened it, I was watching. He got real quiet and left the dining-room table and all the other mail unopened. He walked over, put the paper and the envelope in the fireplace, and burned them. Then he went for a long walk. Let me tell you, that night John was as sweet as he's ever been. And he's been pretty good ever since—that's like five years—until the last couple of months."

Carmen waved her hand, wafting the scent of perfume across the bed. "He's hitting me more now. In the bedroom, so the kids don't know. Couple times I couldn't go out. But what's got me scared is both our girls are teenagers, and he's come real close to hitting them too. If that happens, I've got to leave him. But I don't want to leave if I don't have to. See, I signed a prenup that doesn't give me much to live on, and my lawyer says it will cost a lot to take John to court and we got no guarantees. And if he gets joint custody, then how do I look after my girls when I'm not around?" Carmen paused. "So I wonder maybe if I help you; then you can help me. Charge me your regular rates, of course."

Carmen reached into her purse and pulled out a photocopy. "Here's the copy I made that one day. Maybe you can have somebody go ask him about it without letting him know you got it from me. If it scares him like it did the first time, maybe it'll be another five years before he lays a hand on me. By then my girls will be ready to move out, go to university."

Carmen placed the photocopy in Kellie's hands. "Will you do it?" Carmen asked.

In the office of the antique shop, Glennifer held the phone to her ear and listened briefly.

"This is very kind of you, sir," Glennifer said. Her accent was the peculiar Southern of Charleston, now held mainly by the generation that had not grown up watching television and was therefore untainted by mainstream America. "I've been expecting your call. I'm sorry I was too busy yesterday."

I raised a questioning eyebrow.

"Persistent telemarketer," Elaine whispered to me. "Lightbulbs."

Glennifer held the sheet in front of her, peering down through her reading glasses. "Now, young man, can you please tell me what kind of filaments they have?"

She listened to the answer.

"Is it a CC-9 or just a C-9? . . . Frosted or clear? . . . Thank you, but I really prefer frosted. Do they contain mercury? I'm very concerned about that, you know. Some manufacturers have low-mercury ones. Much better for the planet, wouldn't you agree?"

From our end, it seemed like a monologue, with appropriate pauses.

"Do they contain solder?" Glennifer asked. "Or are they lead-free? I'm sure I've already mentioned my concern for the environment, but we do only have one earth, you know. Is the socket brass or aluminum? . . . Oh, that's too bad. I really prefer brass. Can you get brass in? . . . Do those bulbs have solder? And what's their mercury content? Have these been approved by the Illuminating Engineering Society? . . . Oh, young man, I'm very surprised and disappointed you aren't familiar with IES. I can get you their address if you like. . . . Very well, I won't force it on you. How many foot-candles do these bulbs generate? . . . You do know what a foot-candle is, don't you? Or should I refer you to IES? I see."

Glennifer marked off each question as she went down her list. "How many lumens of output then? . . . Oh, thank you. Can you explain to me what a lumen is? I've been arguing about that with my sister, and it would be nice to have an expert settle it for us. . . . I see. No, wait. She's right here."

Glennifer handed the phone to Elaine. "Oh, thank you, young man," Elaine gushed. "I've been looking forward all day for the chance to talk to someone besides my sister. It can get lonely, you know, when you become a senior. How old are you? . . . You're as young as you sound. I'm not afraid of thirty years' age difference. Are you as handsome as you sound? . . . Don't be so modest. Do you have a girlfriend? Say, I just thought of something. Does your company send anyone over to install the lightbulbs? Would *you* install them for us? We can have ourselves a party. . . . Oh. Well, how many people does it take at your company to change a lightbulb? . . . I see. Please, don't go. We get so lonely. Can you call us tomorrow at the same time? My sister has more questions for you. Hello? Hello?"

Elaine smiled and set the phone down, then burst into girlish laughter. Angel offered a high five. Elaine slapped Angel's palm. Glennifer pretended a scowl, then relented and exchanged high fives with them both.

I took the opportunity to steal Angel's chair. My leg hurt.

"That was as easy as falling into mud, wasn't it?" I said.

"Nicholas Barrett, that is a very ungentlemanly comment," Angel said, imitating Elaine's accent.

"Yeah, Nick," Elaine said, mimicking Angel's voice. "And immature."

I groaned. "I liked it better when you didn't get along."

"We're doing our best to pretend for your sake, Nick," Glennifer said. "After all, you persist in visiting us with her every afternoon."

"Today I have a reason," I said.

Angel didn't give me a chance to explain. She took advantage of Glennifer's friendliness to speak quickly. "That drop-leaf dining table beside the Queen Anne square stool . . . it's a Duncan Phyfe, isn't it? Solid walnut top, accented by a burl walnut apron and drawer front. Finished with brass toes and joined by a trestle for additional support."

Elaine and Glennifer froze, all traces of hilarity instantly gone. This was business now. Even if it came from a twelve-year-old.

"I'd like to buy the table too," Angel said. "Along with the Queen Anne. You know, the stool with waterfall side panels, cabriole legs, and slipper feet."

"You mispronounced *cabriole*," Glennifer snapped. "And why are you trying to impress us with all of that knowledge?"

"You said if I went on the Internet and got you a list of questions about lightbulbs, you would owe me a favor. So I'd like to buy both of those pieces. Maybe with some kind of price break. What do you think, Nick? Isn't that fair?"

"I'm out of this one," I said. "This is between you and these equally respectable women."

Elaine coughed. She pointed to the office door. Glennifer nodded. They stepped outside for a private discussion.

"Angel," I said, "subject change. I've been wanting to ask you something. But I didn't have a chance in the cab."

"Sure, Nick. Fire away."

I tried not to be captivated by the grin on her face as I asked my question. "Tell me, what do you know about a wallet belonging to Miles Ashby?"

Danielle Pederson was Kellie's second visitor that afternoon. She was sixty-eight but looked more than a decade younger, the result of being able to afford the best money could buy in health spas, fitness trainers, clothing, cosmetics, and plastic surgery.

"It took me an hour or so this morning to return your assistant's call," Danielle told Kellie. "After he explained where you were, I booked my flight right after I managed to talk to him. I was so shocked when he explained why you hadn't returned any of my messages."

Danielle sat sideways on her chair, legs pressed together, a habit instilled in her during an era when finishing schools were still in fashion among the rich. She wore a long, red silk skirt and a blouse to match. Her fingers were clustered with gold. Despite the power that money had given her, though, there was an aura of kindness about Danielle. She saw the perspiration beading on Kellie's forehead and leaned forward to wipe it away with a tissue from a nearby box.

"I am so, so sorry this happened to you," Danielle whispered.

Kellie was able to muster a smile. She'd just received another shot of painkiller. She had already discovered how diffi-

cult it was to be expressive in her condition. With the painkiller relaxing her muscles, it was nearly impossible.

"This was a long ways to come," Kellie mumbled, her concentration loosened by the growing euphoria of the opiate.

"Nonsense. I might have made the visit even if I didn't have something new for you. After all, you were such a dear over the last few weeks."

Kellie fought heavy eyelids. "Something new?"

"I did what you suggested. Started looking on my own. And what I found, I believe, is enough for you to start all over again."

It took effort for Kellie to put her thoughts together. "It's going to be a while before I get out of here. . . ."

"Your assistant," Danielle said. "Surely he can begin for you. Remember how urgently I want this taken care of."

Kellie nodded. At least, it felt like a nod. She wasn't tracking her thoughts very clearly. And the last portion of their conversation had become a haze.

"Wonderful," Danielle said. "I'll visit him tonight."

She patted Kellie's hand. "Don't worry. I've got his name and number. And I had one of my secretaries get his address. He and I will take care of it from here."

✛

"Wallet," I repeated.

Angel was rearranging her face to look innocent. "Huh?"

"A thing that holds money," I said. "Credit cards. When people have them stolen, they sometimes go to the police."

"Stolen? Are you trying to tell me something, Nick? Just

because I wasn't born in a big fancy mansion, it doesn't mean that you should just assume—"

"Angel." I said it sternly. We both knew her history.

"Just messing with you," she said. "Yeah, I found a wallet yesterday. In Kellie's hospital room."

"Found it? Funny how no one else noticed it was on the floor."

"Did I say," Angel said, "that I found it on the floor? It was in his jacket."

"So you happened to be looking in his suit jacket?"

She nodded.

"For what?" I asked.

"His wallet. I was mad at him, Nick. How'd I know he was going to come back in and apologize for what he said? By the way, you still haven't explained why he did that. I figured for sure he'd whup you in the hallway."

"Don't change the subject. You looked in his suit jacket for his wallet. That's theft, Angel."

"I said I *found* it," she explained patiently. "I didn't say I *stole* it."

"It's missing," I said. "He reported that to the police."

"Not missing. Just wanted to make him sweat a little. I turned it in to the hospital's lost-and-found department. All his money and credit cards are still there."

Glennifer and Elaine returned.

"We presume," Glennifer said, "that you want those pieces for Nick's house. It's a kind gesture, of course, but those pieces are dreadfully expensive."

Angel gave them her disarming smile. "Don't have to be

73

if you don't want." She smiled again, this time at me. "We're cool on the wallet?"

"We'll talk," I answered. But we were cool on it. I knew her background. Six months earlier, she would have stolen the wallet. Now she'd simply moved it to a place Miles could find it—eventually. When Angel and I talked later, I hoped to bring her closer to understanding why even that action was not pristine. But I'd pick a time for the discussion when it wouldn't put her on the defensive.

Angel led Glennifer away. Leaving me with Elaine.

Finally I had a chance to ask what I needed. "Elaine," I began, "you of anyone would know some of the connections between the old families around here."

"Nick, are you involved in something?"

"Remember Victoria Sebastian?"

"Of course. Poor thing."

"So you've heard the rumors about domestic violence."

"Well founded. Please tell me why you are asking."

"Here's a wild question," I said. "She disappeared in 1978. Twenty years before that—as you may recall from the news stories—Whitman Metiere disappeared. His body was found under the Freemason lodge this year. Any idea what could tie both of those events together?"

Her answer surprised me.

"Please, Nick. Whatever you are doing, leave all of that alone."

The fear on her face surprised me too.

"Elaine?"

She shook her head. "That's all I want to say."

CHAPTER

8

Walking down the hallway to find Angel, I held two overnight envelopes that the housekeepers had received during the day—one from New Jersey, the other from Wyoming—both addressed for priority delivery to Grace Louise Starr.

While I was curious as to their contents and the reason, of course, for those contents, both were unopened. I felt it was important to respect Angel and her privacy the same way I would want to be treated. I would make the packages my business, I had decided, only if they involved Angel in anything that might hurt her or be part of any criminal activity. What frightened me was that very real possibility. Angel was not malevolent by any means, simply opportunistic, but she had a less-than-discerning sense of what differentiated right from wrong.

She was in the kitchen with Maddie; I heard her voice

before I rounded the corner. "I'm going to ask Nick if my packages came in," she said to Maddie, "because now that I've made some money, this is what I want to do."

Money? The overnight packages held checks or cash? I stopped. Despite my noble intentions of giving Angel her privacy, I could not resist this opportunity to eavesdrop.

"I was thinking of getting you a puppy," Angel continued to Maddie. "I always wanted one for me, but now that I'm too grown-up for one, if Nick said it was all right, you would probably love one. A beagle. Definitely a beagle. I always wanted a beagle, so that's maybe the dog for you."

By necessity, this was a monologue. I could picture Maddie holding on to Angel's leg, gazing in different directions with her customary intensity as she listened to her older sister.

"Then I started thinking, Maddie, how lucky we are. Nick's a good guy, you know, and not many kids get to live in a house like this. You should see some of my friends, how bad it is in their homes and how mean their parents are. So I thought that you'd forgive me for spending money on this instead of a puppy. I bought some magnets, and we'll put their photos on the fridge here. We'll send them letters. You'll have to wait until you can write, but if you draw something with crayons, they can have that. See, for what it costs every month to feed a dog, we can help them. . . ."

Silence.

I retraced my steps as quietly as I could, then turned back again, clunking my feet to give as much warning as possible.

I entered the kitchen as Angel stepped away from the fridge. "Hey, Nick."

"Angel—" I waved the overnight envelopes—"these came for you today."

"That's nice." Her tone was one of total disinterest, an interesting contrast to the enthusiasm she'd used in referring to them earlier. "Just some computer stuff. Not a big deal."

"Figured," I said. Although the senders had been individuals, not companies. Although it did not feel like there were any software disks in the packages. Although she'd just referred to money inside them.

I glanced at the fridge, trying to show the same disinterest she so successfully affected about the overnight envelopes.

Then I saw them. Two photos. Set at eye-level height for Maddie.

I squatted.

"It's a pain to have them so low," Angel admitted, "but I want Maddie to be their friend."

"Who are they?"

Angel stood beside me. Since I was squatting, she was able to rest a hand on my shoulder. It was a gesture of trust, and it warmed me. As did the photos. Each of a child younger than Angel.

"Emmanuel Casios and Margarita Estelle," Angel explained. "They live in a poor village in Peru. I got the info off the Internet and signed me and Maddie up to be sponsors."

I turned my head and looked directly into Angel's green eyes.

She peered back anxiously. "It's all right with you, isn't it, Nick?"

"Yeah," I said. "It's all right with me."

✢

I thought later that it's our children who can pierce us with truth when we least expect it. Their teeth have not yet been worn down by the bit of the bridle, and life has yet to burden them beyond what they believe they can carry. While they believe they know so much, they are still willing to learn so much more. They are not afraid of questions.

Anson Hanoway Saffron had his own questions. Questions he only asked his journal. Questions he eventually answered for himself.

This was his journal entry for January 2. In September, less than nine months later, he would enter the Citadel.

Had a strange thought today during math class. I wondered what it was like for Jesus at home when he was my age. Was he expected just to be a carpenter and follow the family tradition? Was he supposed to be the son of the father and nothing else?

Maybe early on he knew he was strange and didn't fit in. Like me. Maybe sometimes he wished he could just be the son of his earthly father.

Did he already know his destiny at a young age? Or did he figure it out as he went? I'll bet people in his town—and Charleston is no different, even if it might have more people—thought he was going nowhere. Saw him as just a carpenter who worked with hammers and a chisel and a saw. He had no wife and kids. No house of his own.

Maybe Jesus and me would have hung out. A couple of losers. But then something happened to him or inside of him, and he decided to break away from what his family wanted. Especially from what his mother wanted.

I wonder what she said when he told her that he was leaving their home, leaving his job, leaving that small town.

Why? she would have asked. (My mother would!)

Sitting in math class, it nearly made me laugh out loud, thinking of what Jesus might have said to her. Perhaps he said he needed to bring the people of Israel closer to God. And by the way, also save mankind.

Not likely.

No matter what he said, his mother would have been shocked. He was a firstborn. Like me. His mother probably doted on him. Like mine does me. Maybe she drove him nuts. Like mine. And I'll bet old Joseph wasn't alive then and that all the other brothers had gone off and gotten married.

Still, there must have come the day when Jesus said to his mother that he had to go. Maybe he didn't tell her why, just that he had to go because he had a destiny *burning inside him that he couldn't explain to anyone until he got there.*

I wonder if I could do that. Tell my mother I'm not going to the Citadel. That I have other dreams even if I don't know what they are yet. I need to find out, to make sense of all that, and I can't do it at the Citadel. I need answers to my questions. Real answers. And I need courage. Like Jesus had.

It must have been something, the day that Jesus gave everything up to follow his dream.

Like Anson, Angel had so much ahead of her, more dreams than even she understood.

I ached for what she didn't know yet. For what she didn't know she didn't know. The hurts that would come.

Was this aching, too, something real parents felt for their children?

⁜

We had been together less than a year, Angel and Maddie and I, but we had already begun to establish an evening ritual that gave us a small sense of family. Preparing the meal was Angel's responsibility; cleanup was mine. I was getting tired of macaroni and cheese or grilled ham and cheese sandwiches or heated canned soup. Angel took such pride in her task, however, that I didn't have the heart to suggest any variations.

Yet. I consoled myself with the fact that her culinary limitations did not lead to massive cleanup tasks.

Also, by my imperial decree, cell phones—mine and Angel's—were powered down during the meal. If calls came in on the landline, neither of us was permitted to answer.

Conversation during the meal, by the same decree, was limited to reporting and analyzing events of the day, discussing hopes or dreams, or even complaining about any persons outside the household. My goal was harmony. And it was only possible because of the officially sanctioned beef time that followed the evening meal.

Each night, after dinner and cleanup were finished, I prepared a pot of tea and a plate of cookies, and the three of us retired to a room where men once used to smoke cigars. There, with Maddie at Angel's feet, Angel and I discussed any domestic problems that either of us had or felt we had. Thus far, it had worked well. I also used this time to read a short passage to them from one of the Gospels—Matthew, Mark, Luke, or John. I didn't intend to force my faith upon them, but I wanted them to hear about Jesus walking the earth among his friends and enemies. Before Angel and Maddie could decide what to believe about him, they needed to know about him.

On this evening I was grateful that Angel had added tuna to her macaroni and cheese. I had just expressed my appreciation for her cooking when the phone rang.

We sat in the kitchen, and the phone and answering machine were on the far counter. I didn't even look over. I wanted Angel to understand that our time together was more important than most other considerations.

When the machine clicked on, we clearly heard the voice of Amelia Layton. "Nick, sorry it took this long to get back to you. I was on shift all day. Call me at home when you get the chance. Hope things are going well."

I took another bite of macaroni.

Maddie, as always, had pushed her chair almost against Angel's. Maddie rarely spoke, just observed. And stayed as close to Angel as possible.

"That was your doctor friend, huh, Nick?" Angel said. She spooned some macaroni into Maddie's mouth. "The one who lives in Chicago. The one you used to date."

I nodded. Then, at a certain point, it had become apparent to us, especially her, that we were not destined to be a good couple.

"She said she was getting back to you," Angel said. "That means you called her today."

"Yes, Angel. Would you mind passing the milk?"

"Didn't she dump you?"

"It's a little more complicated than that. Would you mind passing the milk?"

"What's complicated? She was here to visit for a weekend. She left, and she hasn't been back. To me, that's getting dumped."

"Angel, you might recall there was a lot happening around that time. Someone chasing you, remember? The cult? House fire?" I tapped my chin and pretended I was trying to remember more. "Oh yes. And the painting that started it all."

"So you were dumped."

"You're far too young to have such a strong opinion about these matters. I'd really love some milk."

"Bad move, Nick. Calling her first. She's going to get the wrong idea. That you're weak. That you want her back."

"I believe," I said, thickening my Southern accent to make a parody of it, "that you have now strayed beyond the boundaries of suitable dinner conversation."

"Not a chance, Nick. Events of the day. We can discuss and analyze. You called Amelia. Today. She called you back. Today. Makes it an event I'm discussing and analyzing."

"Milk?" I asked.

"Maybe next time you should come to me for advice before calling a woman. How about you discuss and analyze that?"

I finally took the milk myself and began to fill my glass.

"That's rude, Nick. Reaching across."

"Glad you're learning manners, Angel. And no, I don't want her back. I need her to do me a favor."

"What kind of favor?" Suspicion instantly clouded Angel's face. She stopped with a spoon just short of Maddie's mouth. To her, doctors were part of the official world of social services. "Something about me and Maddie that I should know?"

"It's a favor for Kellie."

"Oh." Angel relaxed but kept the spoon hovering in front of Maddie, who pulled it toward her mouth. Angel seemed unaware of it. "What's with you and Kellie, anyway? She's a looker, Nick. When you going to make a move?"

"Angel . . ." I sighed. "Hey, let's talk about this stool and drop-leaf table you purchased from Glennifer and Elaine. I know you've got money of your own from your grandmother, but I think household furnishings are my responsibility."

"It's funny when you talk so grown up."

"Don't try to change the subject."

Angel smiled. I saw the hint of the woman she would become. Beguiling, devilish, and utterly charming. "Trust me on this, okay?" she said.

Those were Angel's famous words.

I was about to recall for her benefit how much trouble trusting her had gotten me into in the past when the doorbell rang. This, too, I ignored. The arrangement with our live-in housekeepers was for them to answer during mealtime. Mostly, callers were tourists with questions.

I was surprised, then, when the kitchen door swung open a minute later.

"Mr. Barrett," Ingrid said. Hank, her husband, stood behind her. Both in their sixties, patient and kind, they were wonderful housekeepers. Their natural reserve had made our conversations minimal so far, but gradually we were getting to know each other as more than employer and employees. "There's a woman caller for you. Very insistent that she see you now."

A few minutes later, after the necessary introductions, Danielle Pederson sat opposite me in the front room of the house, with various Barretts of preceding generations glowering down upon her from dim oil paintings.

She told me the story about her son's disappearance in a matter-of-fact tone that matched her air of detached confidence. However, she wasn't a good enough actress to hide the pain in her eyes. Money buys a lot, I'd found out in my lifetime, but it can't erase memories.

On a Saturday night in 1978, three months away from graduating from the Citadel with highest honors, senior cadet Matthew Pederson stood up with his supper dishes and said good-bye to his friends at the mess table. He set the dishes on a tray with other collected dishes and walked to his dorm room for a night of solitary study.

Other cadets recalled seeing him walking down the hall and shutting the door behind him.

It was the last he would be seen for a quarter of a century.

In the weeks after his disappearance, police investigators tried to find the slightest trace of the rest of his actions that evening. When they were unsuccessful, they settled on the theory that Matthew had simply walked away from the Citadel and found a new life under a different name.

His parents refused to believe it. They hired private investigators who came up with no more results but a different conclusion. The private investigators thought it unlikely that Matthew would turn his back on the accolades awaiting him upon graduation or that Matthew would voluntarily reject the wealth that came with his family entitlement.

Matthew's father—who died a decade later of a heart attack—was a Wall Street tycoon in the old-fashioned sense. Expensive suits, expensive cigars, expensive expense accounts. The Pedersons had a Park Avenue condominium in New York City, a large beach house in Miami, and a property in Vail, Colorado: all of these were enticing playgrounds for a young man of Matthew's looks, early accomplishments, and financial stature.

It seemed ridiculous to assume that Matthew would abandon all of this to live somewhere else with a different identity.

Except.

The last week of Matthew's time at the Citadel had been darkened by sudden and growing rumors of his romantic involvement with an older married woman who waited off campus in a taxi to take him away for hours at a time. This, too, his parents refused to believe. In the end, they were torn by conflicting hopes. If the police were correct and Matthew had indeed simply run away, then at least he was still alive. But if he was still alive, then it meant he had rejected them and all they stood for as parents.

If he'd been murdered, however, as they feared, they wanted justice as the only possible consolation. So they continued to hire private investigators until, about a year later, it appeared there was no chance of locating their missing son.

Finally, they had given up hope of finding him, alive or dead. Until a month ago, when Danielle Pederson had received a phone call. One that had led her to Kellie Mixson.

And because of that phone call, Matthew's mother had stepped into my home to ask for the help that Kellie Mixson could not continue to give.

✛

"You might already have known all this," Danielle Pederson said. "If so, I apologize. I'm not aware of how much Miss Mixson has kept you informed of the investigation."

I did know it already. I had talked with Kellie. Kellie had

then e-mailed me her files. Along with a note that said it was not necessary for me to do this extra work. I did not tell this to Danielle Pederson. "Kellie prefers to work independently," was all I said.

"Of course." A polite way of saying she understood that I had not given an answer.

Danielle had been playing with her purse in her lap. It was red and matched her dress. She'd been clasping and unclasping it, the small clicks punctuating her words. She stopped as she leaned forward in her chair and made sure I met her gaze as directly as she met mine. "I sense reluctance," she said.

"I'm just not sure that I can help. In general it seems I am capable of disappointing enough people without making promises."

"I'm not sure you can help either," Danielle said. "I'm a careful woman, Mr. Barrett. I stopped by your house earlier, and your housekeeper said you wouldn't be available until this evening. You can imagine my curiosity, discovering that an assistant to a one-woman investigation agency lives in a house like this. So I called back my own assistant to do some quick background on you. You misrepresented yourself this morning on the phone. Please don't take that as an accusation but as a statement of fact."

"I'm helping a friend who nearly died in a horrible car accident," I said. "She had a backlog of calls. Please don't take that as a defense but as a statement of fact."

She smiled, her first real smile since I'd greeted her ten minutes earlier.

Angel appeared in the doorway of the front room where
Danielle and I sat. She carried a tray of tea and smiled shyly. I
tried not to show my surprise. Angel had changed from jeans
and sweatshirt into an elegant beige dress that I was not aware
she owned. It made her look younger and older at the same
time.

Angel set down the tray. "Cream or sugar?" she asked
Danielle.

"Angel," I said, "this is Mrs. Pederson. She's here from
New York."

Angel extended a hand. "Grace Louise Starr. I'm very
happy to meet you."

Again, I hid surprise. At Angel's obvious effort at manners
and her formality.

Maddie came running into the room and clutched at
Angel's hip. She, too, wore a dress that I didn't know existed in
this household. One that matched Angel's. Angel had put a
bow in Maddie's dark hair. It made my heart ache to see how
beautiful both were.

"This is my sister," Angel said. "Madison. But Madison
doesn't say much."

"Very pleased to meet you both," Danielle answered.
"And yes, I would love some cream and sugar in my tea."

Angel curtsied. Actually curtsied. I pretended this was
normal, for to do otherwise would have mortified and humiliated Angel. She poured the tea and added the necessities.
Then smiled and departed with Maddie following.

"Are they your children?" Danielle Pederson smiled to
blunt the directness of her question. "You can understand my

curiosity, of course. And I'm old enough now that I indulge it freely and without embarrassment."

I was about to explain that I was their guardian, but I realized there was only one answer to her question. "Yes," I said. "They are my children. I'm very proud of them."

"Matthew was our only child. We were very proud of him too. Will you at least listen to what I have to say before making a decision whether or not to help me?"

"That sounds fair," I said.

"Let me begin by telling you something very painful. It is not public knowledge and I insist that it remain out of public knowledge. That's one of the main reasons I went to a private investigation agency." Danielle looked at me expectantly.

I obliged by nodding.

"My son's body was among those found last January," she said slowly. "Among the others unearthed here in Charleston beneath the Freemason lodge."

CHAPTER

9

Officially, the police department maintained that there was no connection between the seven bodies and the Freemasons of Charleston. The crawl space was accessible from the outside of the building—as the media had consistently and repeatedly been told—so whoever had placed the bodies there had taken advantage of this accessibility. Furthermore, it was very likely the spot had been chosen because it would cast suspicion on an organization the public would want to believe had some involvement. It was a classic red herring, the department said, a distraction from finding out exactly who had placed the bodies there.

The *unofficial* position among the team of detectives assigned to the case, as Jubil told me, was much different.

While the public only knew that Whitman Metiere's body had been identified, over the last month the police had made four other positive identifications. Three of them had been prominent Charlestonians.

Arnold Rathbone, circuit court judge, had disappeared at age fifty-nine on October 31, 1923. Malcolm Abernathy, a shipping businessman, had disappeared on October 31, 1942, at age forty-three. Michael Deveraux, principal at one of Charleston's elite private schools, had disappeared on October 31, 1985, at age twenty-seven.

It was eerie enough that the three men had been victims in three separate decades spanning over half a century; including Whitman Metiere, that meant four victims over four different decades. If this had been a serial killing, why were the murders so far apart, and what were the motivations? More eerie that the obvious link among all four men was the date of their disappearance—Halloween night.

Most eerie of all, however, was the final link. As with Whitman Metiere, the last known destination of each of the other three had been the chaotic frenzy of the All Hallows' Eve masquerade ball at the Metiere mansion south of Broad.

That made it all the more puzzling that the remains in one of the other caskets belonged to a college senior, who had gone missing from his dorm in the Citadel in 1978.

Matthew Pederson.

Who most definitely had not attended the All Saints' Ball.

I found it revealing how quickly Jubil arrived after I paged him asking about Matthew Pederson's body.

Shortly after 9 A.M., ten minutes after I'd called in the page, he found me where I'd told him he could find me. White Point Gardens.

I was sitting on a bench in the shade of the trees. White Point Gardens is significant to Charleston because here a battery of cannons had protected the city against the invasions of the War of Secession and later the War of Northern Aggression. The first we'd won; the second we had not. Cannons still stood in the park, their barrels plugged with concrete.

Jubil pulled up in his unmarked Chevrolet and parked illegally in front of a fire hydrant. I doubted his car would be towed. I commented on that when he stood in front of me, hands on his hips, face set in stone. He wore khaki pants, a black mock turtleneck, and a black cashmere sports jacket. Hip.

"Maybe you could get the department to cover what it cost me when my Jeep was towed yesterday," I said. "Because now it appears I was on police business too."

"Listen," he said, "I want to know how you found out about Matthew Pederson, and I want to know right now."

" 'Cause what sticks out," I continued, "is that any work I do on the Victoria Sebastian case is more than likely related to the little treasure trove of bodies in the Freemason burial grounds."

"Whoever the leak is, I'm going to find that person. And they're going to be in as much pain as I intend to inflict on you for going behind my back to department sources."

"Your upper lip has a tic when you're angry," I said. "Interesting. But here's the situation. I've got a voice recording that links Victoria Sebastian to those bodies under the Freemason lodge. Now it turns out that Matthew Pederson was under the lodge too. That's enough to connect them, don't you think? So anything I do in searching for what happened to Sebastian is directly related to police work. And if I'm doing police work, I ought to be able to park where I want, when I want." I smiled, knowing his anger was building. "Just like you, Jubil. I ought to be able to pull up in front of a fire hydrant and—"

"Enough." He slipped off his sunglasses, tucked an earpiece inside the collar of his mock turtleneck, and folded his arms. "This is not a game."

"You're right," I said. I stood. "But it's fun watching you."

"Be fun watching you sit in a jail cell for obstruction if you don't tell me how you learned about Matt Pederson."

"Let's trade. You tell me what else the department has been keeping from the public about those bodies. Then I'll tell you about Matt."

"No trade. You talk."

I let his glare bounce off me.

"We're talking a murder investigation here," Jubil said in response to my bland lack of reaction. "You don't have any idea how difficult I can make it on you."

My cell phone was in my front pocket. I pulled it out and, still meeting his glare, dialed a number.

"Charleston, please," I said after a few seconds. "The number for the *Post and Courier*." I smiled at Jubil as I waited for directory to connect me. "See, when a private citizen learns something of public interest, that private citizen is almost bound by duty to get the media involved. What I suggest is that you buy me breakfast as we trade information. Otherwise, I might have to make the same deal with a reporter."

He growled his disgust as he grabbed my cell phone and snapped it shut. "I suppose you're going to order steak and eggs, aren't you? The most expensive thing you can find on the menu."

"Seems only fitting. Same thing you did to me yesterday."

The night before, Danielle had given me more information.

After Kellie had turned in a report that added very little to what Danielle already knew, Danielle had paid a visit to someone she hadn't seen in roughly twenty years. Matthew's former fiancée, who had married a condo developer.

Danielle had begun the conversation very bluntly. "Matthew's body has been found. I am not able at this point to tell you how or where it was found. But I wanted you to hear it from me. That, after all these years, it was found."

They sat on a balcony of the penthouse suite in an ocean-side high-rise.

"Are you sure?" Cheryl Harper paused. "I mean is he actually . . . ?"

"Dead? You can say it now. Matthew is dead." Danielle smiled sadly. "Strangely enough, once I finally said it out loud, it became real. I was able to start mourning him."

"He's dead," Cheryl whispered. She was blonde and, at ten in the morning, still in a robe. She was in her midforties and had worked hard to look a decade younger. She'd had Botox injections a week earlier, and the wrinkles on her forehead were faint, frozen creases that did not respond to the movement on the rest of her face.

"In all likelihood, it was murder," Danielle said. Another sad smile. "Which was much, much more difficult to say aloud the first time. But once I did, it too became real. Real enough that I am very, very angry about it. That's why I'm here. With some questions. For you."

"It's been twenty-five years since he and I were engaged, Mrs. Pederson. My oldest son is now the age he was at the Citadel."

"And if your son went missing tomorrow, wouldn't you want as many answers as possible? Perhaps from his girlfriend or fiancée? Perhaps like the answers that I believe you denied me twenty-five years ago?"

Cheryl tightened her robe as she stared at the untouched glass of iced tea on the tray beside her patio chair. There was a long silence.

"Cheryl." Danielle spoke firmly. "When I told you he was dead, you were surprised. You had questions about where he'd been found. But when I told you he'd been murdered, you didn't have any questions. That tells me a lot. What did you keep from me? From the police?"

More silence.

"I believe," Danielle said, "that I could make things difficult for you. That I could arrange for the police to ask you the same questions now. That even if you refused to speak or continued to lie about what you know, that someday when the truth is known, you could even face legal repercussions, large or small, depending on what you've kept hidden."

"Don't threaten me. I come from a family with money too. I can hire legal help just as good as yours."

"I have no intention of doing that. I was merely outlining an option that I have no intention of using. I don't want to force you to tell me or the police. In fact, if you send me away right now, you won't hear from me again. No, I will not try to force you. But I am begging you. I'm an old woman. Desperate to find some kind of closure on the most horrible event of my life. My son. Gone without a trace."

Cheryl let out a long breath. "Back then, when he disappeared, I thought my silence was protecting him. I'd promised him that. He wanted to escape the Citadel and all his troubles there."

"But your engagement . . ."

"We were having major troubles. That was one of the secrets I kept from you. Two days before he disappeared, I told him we were through. He begged me not to tell anyone for a month. He hoped to be able to change my mind before the month was up."

"Why did you break it off?"

"You'll laugh when I tell you this. It's so preposterous; it was another reason I kept quiet."

"I won't laugh." Danielle spoke in a low voice. "Nothing about this is funny."

"Look around us," Cheryl said. "They say the best things in life are free. Like sunsets. No, it costs money to enjoy the sunset. Especially from up here. Down there, it's crowded. Tourists fighting for room to get the best view. Street people too busy scratching out an existence to stop and look. And how can anyone enjoy a sunset when they're worried about the next mortgage payment, the price of gasoline? I believe only the rich enjoy life. I was born into a rich family, just like Matthew. Unlike Matthew, I intended to hold on to my birthright. He wanted . . ."

Cheryl paused to sip her iced tea. She squinted and grimaced, as if it had been spiked. Perhaps it had. "This is what's preposterous. Matthew wanted to give it all up. Become a missionary."

"Missionary!"

"Africa. The inner city of Chicago. Didn't matter. He said life would only have meaning if he turned his back on family wealth. I told him that was unacceptable. If he wanted me for his wife, *this* was the life we would live. Miami in the fall and winter, southern France in the summer."

"Missionary." Danielle tried out the word—in the same way she'd had to say *dead* and *murdered* to believe both events were real. "I'm not laughing. But it sounds so unlike him."

"He'd changed. I think it was everything that happened in the months before. With a freshman they couldn't break. Over the phone, he used to tell me the stories. The things he and three other seniors had done to him. We'd both laughed so hard we couldn't breathe. Then . . ."

"Yes?"

"Then one day it wasn't funny to Matthew anymore," Cheryl said. "He said something terrible had happened. Said he wanted out of the Citadel and was going to make it up to God by becoming a missionary. Said he had a vision. Said . . ." She paused again. "Said he'd been born again. To a life

committed to Jesus. I'm all for church and everything, but he
wanted to go way overboard. I told him I wasn't going to follow
him into the jungle."

When Cheryl stopped speaking, it was Danielle's turn for
a long silence as she tried to absorb all of it. Cheryl reached for
a tube of suntan lotion beside her chair and began to coat her
arms and legs. "It's a tough balance. A person wants enough
tan to look healthy, but too much tan is bad for the skin."

"Don't move on to trivialities," Danielle said quietly.
"Please talk to me. What terrible thing happened?"

"I don't know. He wouldn't say. Told me he and his three
friends had sworn a pact of secrecy to protect themselves. And
when he disappeared, I thought he was running away from that
trouble to live a life of poverty. I didn't want any part of that,
but if that's what he'd decided, I was at least going to protect
him by keeping all of that to myself."

"I think," Danielle said, "by then he was beyond the need
for protection. Please, is there something more than iced tea in
that glass?"

Cheryl smiled sheepishly. "Somewhere in the world it's
cocktail time."

"I need some of it."

Cheryl handed Danielle the glass. Danielle took a long,
hard drink.

"Are you able to tell me the names of his friends?"
Danielle asked. "The three you mentioned? And who this poor
freshman was and what they'd done to him?"

Cheryl nodded. And told Danielle Pederson all that she
remembered.

✠

"Anson Hanoway Saffron," I said. "Name ring a bell?"

"Yeah," Jubil said. "Even though we were barely teenagers then. Kid who committed suicide at the Citadel."

Except for a couple of businessmen sitting on the stools at the counter, most of the morning rush was already gone from the Sweetwater Café. Jubil and I sat in our usual booth by the window.

I was about to answer, but our waitress stopped at our table and poured our coffee. I ordered the steak and eggs, just to make Jubil grimace.

"Anson Hanoway Saffron," I said. Some Charlestonians from older families had a peculiar habit of using last names as first names. "His mother, Isabelle Hanoway, married into the Saffron family. She was the last of the Hanoways. Rich and well respected, especially in the forties, did contract stuff for the Navy. Then the family business almost tanked in the early fifties but recovered after a big loan bailed it out. Still, Isabelle's father, Anson Hanoway Saffron's maternal grandfather, committed suicide shortly after. Seemed strange, since his business was fine."

"Apple don't fall far from the tree, huh? 'Course, suicide is a difficult trait to pass on if you do it as a teenager. But what does this have to do with the Pederson kid? I'm telling you, whoever leaked this—"

"Here's the link. Keep in mind I got it—and the Hanoway family history—from reliable sources."

"Someone in the department."

"Let it go, Jubil. I had to call Glennifer and Elaine this morning to get this background."

"Oh," he said, giving me his first smile of the morning. "Definitely reliable."

"The big loan that bailed out the Hanoway family business? Came from Whitman Metiere. Two things in common with Matt Pederson. Metiere's body found in the same place as Pederson's. Both linked to the Hanoway family."

"Linked to the Hanoway family?"

"You do a bad job of pretending innocence, Jubil. If you guys knew that Matt Pederson was in one of the coffins, you also know that he was part of the Citadel inquiry into Anson Hanoway Saffron's suicide."

Jubil's face became angry again. "There's no way you learned that from Glennifer and Elaine."

"I want what you know on the other bodies under the Freemason lodge. Then you get how I found out about Pederson."

He blew across his cup of coffee to cool it. "There's some bizarre stuff here, Nick."

That's when he told me the identities of the other three men. The nights they had disappeared. And the fact that each of them, like Whitman Metiere, had last been seen at the All Saints' Ball.

"We're desperate to keep a lid on it," Jubil continued. "If the media gets ahold of it, all of a sudden Charleston becomes a media zoo. From network news crews to tabloids. It's the last thing we want. If the case is solved, we present the hard cold facts and keep the storm to a minimum."

"If?" I poured cream into my coffee.

"Nick, we've identified five of the seven bodies. As near as the forensic experts can pin it, the two remaining bodies have been under the Freemason lodge for nearly a century. How much chance do you think we have of finding out who did them?"

I whistled. "Some kind of persistent serial killer. Think of the fun the tabloids will have with that."

"Be nice if people thought it was all one person responsible. But the obvious conclusion is the one we've taken great pains to keep the press from using to sell papers."

"That it's not a person," I said. "An organization."

"Look, there are more than a few influential members of the lodge. Citywide. Statewide—"

I finished it for him. "Nationwide."

"Presidential circles," Jubil said. "All legit, I'm sure. So legit that the heat is on to make sure nothing from this plays into conspiracy theories."

"Good," I said. "Gives me some clout." I let that sink in as I paused to take my first drink of coffee.

He raised an eyebrow.

"How were the men killed?" I asked.

"I can't tell you that."

"I have five syllables for you," I said. I enunciated each one slowly and clearly. *"Post and Courier."* I made a motion of clubbing downward. My clout. Threatening to call the newspaper.

"Really," he said, "I can't tell you that. Because I'm not able. The two oldest bodies are skin and bone and hair. Our forensic experts have found nothing on the bones that show any sign of violence."

"And Matthew Pederson?"

"Same thing," he said. "No signs of violence on the bones."

Our waitress approached again. The Sweetwater Café served decent food and served it fast.

"Your turn. So how'd you find out about Matt?"

I told him about Danielle Pederson's visit. How she'd recorded her conversation with Cheryl Harper, then had it transcribed.

"So his mother's learned something more?" Jubil carefully cut his steak into a dozen pieces. That was an idiosyncrasy of his: getting the entire plate ready so that once the food had cooled, he could eat it one bite after another without wasting time to cut it. "But why come to you?"

"Kellie Mixson worked the case for her when your department first told Danielle Pederson that Matthew's body had been identified among the seven. Now that Kellie's unable to help, Danielle's turned to me. She thinks I'm Kellie's assistant."

"That doesn't explain why the Pederson woman went to a detective agency in the first place. We have department guys on it."

"Seems the department didn't do much good when he first disappeared, and seems to be making little progress on it now. You know her background. New York and Miami social-ite. Second and third cousin to highly placed Democrats. She told me how the tabloids had made her life absolute misery when Matthew first disappeared. She wants the truth about him. She'll take that truth and present it to some of the respected journals. They'll play the story the way she wants it. Until then, she's terrified this will leak somehow and the tabloids will start to play with headlines."

Jubil pointed his knife at me. "Which is why I freaked when you told me about Matthew. We've been promised we'll lose our badges if his name gets out. That's the kind of political power in D.C. that her relatives have. But I don't know why she trusts you."

"I think she sees no choice. How many listed private investigators does Charleston have?"

"Including Kellie?"

"Including Kellie."

"You've made your point," Jubil said.

Including Kellie, the answer was two.

"Danielle went to her first," I explained. "Kellie came away with hardly anything new. Said she couldn't help Danielle unless Danielle found anything else."

"And she found something else?"

I nodded.

"What?" Jubil was focused on me.

"Can't tell you anything more," I said. "Client confidentiality."

"You're not a PI!"

I shrugged. "Call me a freelance journalist then. Trying to write an article for a one-person audience."

"Nick, I'm warning you."

"She doesn't want cops going around asking questions about Saffron and the Citadel. If that gets back to the media, it's her old tabloid nightmare all over again. Except worse, because now they'll be able to tie in a hundred-year-old serial killing with the suicide of a fellow Citadel cadet."

"You can't withhold information. This is a murder investigation."

"So I've been told." I smiled upward at our waitress, accepted more coffee. "Jubil, there's one other thing. Danielle Pederson has upped the ante. She's offered a hundred grand for the truth behind her son's death. I'm pretty sure Kellie can use that money. She might not be able to work for three months."

"Knight in shining armor," Jubil said. "Saving the damsel in distress."

"Just helping a friend in need."

"You're really going to keep what she told you to yourself?"

"All I need to do is visit two of Matthew's old friends and ask them questions. That was my promise to her. No more than that. If I find something that leads to who killed him, Kellie's agency gets the bonus Danielle Pederson promised."

Jubil spoke very quietly. "I wish you'd leave this alone, Nick. All of those different people were killed over different decades. Matthew didn't disappear on Halloween night like the others, but his coffin still held the same thing that the other seven held."

"A body," I said, trying to be funny.

Jubil continued as if I hadn't interrupted. "On top of the bones and hair," he said. "Laid on top of the body. Each had the same thing." He paused. "This is not for anyone else but you. Not even Kellie. Not even Danielle. I find out you told anyone, it'll put a big dent in our friendship. And I'm only telling you because maybe it will convince you to leave this alone, buy an antique shop, and do something useful instead of playing detective. Go live a long happy life with Angel and Maddie and your old lady friends."

"Word of honor. I won't tell."

"Nick, all of them were found with a small cross in their coffins." He took a napkin and sketched it out for me.

It looked like the one Kellie had seen the day before in the hospital. The one Carmen Sebastian had hoped Kellie might use to force John Sebastian to stop beating Carmen and her daughters.

C H A P T E R

10

I watched Kellie as she slept. And felt a slight twinge of guilt for doing so. Her face was relaxed of pain and showed the vulnerability that comes with the innocence of sleep.

I wanted to lean forward and brush some of the hair back from her eyes. But that intimacy—slight as it might be—was not part of our friendship. She and I had met because of Angel, and Angel's welfare was our common ground.

In the weeks before the car accident, Kellie and I had begun to work out together at a local gym. I avoided the treadmill, of course, but did what cardiovascular I could on the bikes. She'd shown me some weight-lifting techniques, and we took turns spotting each other on the bench.

We were careful to keep our time together as buddy-buddy. Eight months earlier, her longtime boyfriend had moved to California to pursue screenwriting, and she'd told me that flatly, making it plain that further discussion about that subject was not welcome. I had no idea why she had not gone out there with him, why they hadn't yet married, or if she even wanted the relationship to continue.

I'd been married very young, but the marriage had been annulled. Since returning to Charleston, I had been in a relationship that I'd wished might continue. It hadn't. And that woman was the caller when my cell phone rang. Loudly. I wasn't able to get to it before Kellie opened her eyes and blinked.

"Phone tag is over," Amelia Layton said to me. "Finally caught up with you."

Kellie struggled to sit up, propping herself on her elbows.

"You're doing fine?" I asked Amelia.

"Is that a personal question?"

"Only if you want it to be," I said.

"Sure. I'm doing more than fine. Got engaged last week."

I tried to decide how I felt. Set aside the question. "Congratulations."

"You sound like you mean it."

"I do," I said, trying to figure out if I did.

Kellie frowned, wondering about the identity of my caller. I covered the mouthpiece and whispered Amelia's name to her.

"Well, it happened fast," Amelia continued on the other end of the phone. "But sometimes when you know it's the right thing . . ."

Unspoken was the implication, *Ours wasn't.*

"Anyway," she said quickly, as if realizing how I might interpret her previous words, "I did pull a few strings for you. It's the least I could do."

Once again, she paused as if realizing the unspoken. *The least she could do after it didn't work out with us.*

And once again, she hurried on. "Had the hospital in Charleston fax me all the records you wanted me to check. I'm not even going to ask why you wanted to know about this Victoria Sebastian. It's not my business. Nor do I want it to be."

I caught the drift of that too. She disapproved of the fact that I was looking into something that appeared not to be any of my business. Which, on a different matter, was what had driven her away from me earlier.

"I'm going to give you the short of it," Amelia said. The cell phone crackled slightly. "It's crazy as usual around here."

Here was the emergency department of her hospital.

"I'm ready," I said.

"Victoria Sebastian made repeated trips to the hospital in the years you asked about. Then, shortly after the death of her son, no more visits."

"Death of her son?"

"Isn't that why you asked me to get the family's medical records?"

"Yes. I just didn't expect—"

"He died at age three." Even with the shaky connection, I could tell she was angry. "Nick, doctors today viewing the autopsy would strongly suspect shaken baby syndrome. I can make a report, you know. Have the parents try to explain, even now after all this time has passed."

"The mother disappeared," I said. "A long time ago. The father has remarried. Easy for him to put the blame on her."

"Either way, I hate this. You'd think I would get used to it. But I don't."

"Thanks for your help. Any chance you can fax me those reports?"

"Sorry. Doing what I did bent enough rules. You'll have to get them through proper channels."

"I understand."

More crackling as we each paused.

"Nick," she said.

Her serious tone quickened my heart. That's when I discovered I wasn't all that happy for her and her recent engagement.

"Yes," I answered.

"You didn't ask me about the baby girl. Sophia Sebastian."

"Oh."

"She was only one at the time of her last medical examination. There were no more. But the records show suspicious injuries. Classic child abuse. I guess I lied to you when I said I don't care. I do. If you can get the person who would do that to a child, I'd like to hear about it later."

"Sure. At your wedding, huh?"

"No, Nick. Call me or write me with the news. You won't be getting an invitation."

She hung up the phone.

I had a lot to report to Kellie.

An hour earlier, I'd driven to the Mount Carmel African Methodist Episcopal Church on Bradley Street, well north of

Broad. This was a neighborhood of boarded-up windows, obscene graffiti splashed across faded billboards, and rusting cars parked along sidewalks with weeds sprouting through the cracks of the concrete.

The Mount Carmel church, however, was like the flame of a candle in a dark corner. Although it was an old wooden structure built by freedmen over a hundred years earlier, the building had been kept in good repair. The shingles were shiny black in contrast to the faded, weather-beaten shingles of the buildings on each side. Its walls were freshly painted, a white that almost seemed to glow in the bright October sunshine. The parking-lot lines had been recently painted, and the small lawn on the side and front was as manicured as any mansion's south of Broad.

This was the church my mother had attended when I was a boy, during the years that she'd been ostracized by the wealthy white community where I'd been raised. Then, it had been a church of joyful hallelujahs and a simple trust in God, uncomplicated by seminary-bred theologies. It was the same now, something I knew firsthand, for it was the church I had recently begun attending again, with a deep appreciation for the acceptance I felt among its members.

It was a church where congregation members raised their hands and Bibles and shouted "Amen" and "Praise the Lord" whenever the speaker held them in rapt attention, and where members fanned themselves and murmured "Hep him, Jesus" whenever the speaker faltered or became boring. It was a church where I could sing enthusiastically during the old-time hymns, confident that my painfully out-of-tune voice would be

lost in the swell of praise. It was a church where Angel and
Maddie felt as much at home as I did. A church that had had
the same pastor since my mother attended. Samuel Thorpe.

He was in his office, reading a Bible with the help of a
magnifying glass, when I entered.

I said nothing.

He turned the page, a slow movement of his hand,
accompanied by the crisp sound of onionskin flipping.

Samuel was a vigorous man for someone in his eighties.
He had a habit of running his hands over his bald, egg-shaped
head, as if it still held the hair it had when he was a young man
of fifty. He wore thick glasses that gave him an owlish appearance, and his smile was simply beautiful—an odd way to
describe a man's feature but very apt.

"Nicholas," he said in his deep voice, "it is always a pleasure."

"Please," I said, "don't get up."

I knew the effort would tax him. It always amazed me, the
strength of his voice whenever he spoke from the pulpit.
Mostly, these days, guest speakers came in and Pastor Samuel
gave the prayers during Sunday services. He was well past the
age of retiring, but it was as unthinkable for him as for his
extended family, the congregation that he had been shepherd-
ing for over forty years. I took a chair opposite his desk.

He poured coffee from a thermos into a guest cup and
handed it across to me. "Well," he said, "are you making progress at the archives?"

"Some."

"Your client is not too demanding?"

"So far, Angel is content with what I can bring her," I said. "But the further back I go, the less I want to tell her. It's too shameful. Do I really want to tell her about a great-grandfather who was whipped for stealing a chicken to feed his family? Or tell her about life as a free person of color?"

"Shameful to who, Nick?"

I gave him the answer although we both knew what it would be. "My ancestors."

"Won't help to hide that from her," Samuel said softly. "She won't blame you."

I grimaced. Angel called herself a *mochachino,* because that's how her mother and grandmother had described her. It was a term of love and much more beautiful than *mulatto,* which was a derivative of the Spanish *mula,* or mule, a cross between a mare and a donkey.

And also a beast of burden.

In the rural South in the last half of the 1800s, three out of every four mulattos were slaves. Nearly without fail, the white parentage came from the father's side; had a black man been intimate with a white woman, he would have been hung from the nearest tree. The white fathers usually deserted the children conceived by black slave women, who were in no position to refuse the owner's advances. They deepened the neglect by allowing these unacknowledged children to remain slaves. Sometimes, however, a white father wrote the mulatto child's freedom into his will, and just as often as not, the revelation of children outside the marriage was a shock to the surviving white family members. Either way, it was left up to the white family to complete the job of abandonment begun by the father, forcing the mulatto children off the property to fend for themselves.

I dreaded describing this to Angel because—except for the slavery—it was too close to her own story. Her father—white—had deserted her and her mother while Angel was a baby. She had not seen or heard of him since, didn't even have a photo of him.

Only a century and a half earlier, in the same situation, Angel would have been an abandoned slave child. Or, if acknowledged and liberated from slavery, she would have been forced to wear a metal tag inscribed with these words: *City of Charleston, FREE.* She would have been labeled during a South Carolina state census as a free person of color—an FPC, as they were commonly known. Stuck between two races.

"Nick," Samuel said, "tell it to her up front. Make no apologies or judgment. Let *her* decide what to think about the facts." He stared at me through the Coke-bottle lenses of his spectacles. "But you didn't come here for that, did you? A weekday visit can only mean one thing. You want access to my considerably long memory, don't you?"

"I'm trying to help Kellie."

Sam knew she was in the hospital and why, but he didn't know the last two days' events. I explained.

"I see," he said. He got up and slowly paced his office. He stopped and pulled a book off the shelves that lined one wall. He flipped through it without reading it and replaced it. "You may recall how I advised you to be up front with Angel," he finally said, leaning against his desk. "It's time for me to take my own advice and be up front with you."

I nodded, wondering why he was so reluctant to talk.

"It's a fine line," Samuel said, "between ministering and tending another man's business. I'm generally averse to offering advice unasked for and, always so conscious of my own shortcomings, loath to take notice of another's. You'll bear that in mind as I speak."

"Certainly."

"It's a ticklish business to be friends with a woman, particularly one like Miss Kellie. She's fine-looking and smart and of good character. I'm certain you're not blind to that. I doubt, for that matter, that it's escaped her notice that a woman could do worse than land a man like you. But as you mentioned, she's in a committed relationship, Nick."

"Yes, I have mentioned that before," I said. "But I don't see how this is an issue we need to discuss."

"It's not only an issue of honor," he said, "but of the slow or fast erosion of your soul. Every moral decision you make, Nick, affects your soul. This woman, I can tell, has a hold on you. Don't do anything to hurt her. Her boyfriend. Or you."

Sam straightened and began pacing again. "Now, I'm not suggesting that you have or intend to do anything inappropriate. But it's like driving a car. Good drivers aren't the ones who can handle a car in a skid and keep it on the road. Good drivers are those who recognize when conditions are bad and take action not to get into trouble in the first place."

"Kellie's in trouble," I said. "She needs help. That's all I'm doing."

"You don't have to justify your motives to me. Just beware

of them yourself. All I'm saying is if there's trouble way up the road, it'd be a lot better for you to see it coming and slow down before you reach it."

"Sam, that advice isn't necessary."

"No? Good. Because what you do or don't do impacts more than you now. There's Angel and Maddie."

"Sam!"

"Good," he said. "Get angry. It's an honest emotion. And you have a bad habit of keeping all your emotions hidden."

"Thanks," I said dryly. "Anything else?"

"See how quick you put it back inside?"

"World-class quick," I said. "It's an art."

He sighed at my stubbornness and rubbed the top of his bald head. "How is it I can help you and Miss Kellie this morning?"

I offered him a piece of paper, folded in half. It was the photocopy of the cross symbol that Carmen Sebastian had given to Kellie, the same cross that had been found with seven bodies in seven caskets hidden beneath the lodge.

"In all your years in Charleston," I asked, "have you seen this before?"

Sam opened it. And closed it quickly. "Oh, Nick," he said. "Not this."

"Amelia," Kellie confirmed when I hung up the cell phone and stared at the wall.

I'd been thinking about Amelia. About Kellie's boyfriend.

About Samuel's advice to look ahead at what might be coming up the road.

"Looked into medical records for us. Victoria Sebastian. I'll be able to add that to the report."

"Sounds like Amelia's getting married."

"She is. From what she told me, it looks like my interview yesterday with Dr. Osier paid off. Amelia says the records show definite domestic violence." I reached for the tray of hospital food that Kellie had left untouched. "Mind if I have your Jell-O?"

"Go ahead." Kellie pushed her hair off her forehead. "So how do you feel about it?"

"Angry, of course."

"I don't blame you."

"The baby girl had been abused. Sophia. She was only one. And the boy? Amelia says in all likelihood it was a case of shaken baby syndrome."

"Nick. I meant how do you feel about her upcoming wedding?"

I gulped down the cube of Jell-O in one mouthful. I'd always had a weakness for it, even lukewarm off a hospital tray.

"The wedding. You probably heard me congratulate her," I said. "A detective like you could probably infer that I think it's great."

"Funny how your voice manages to convey heartfelt enthusiasm."

"Funny how you're showing a lot more interest than I expected for something so trivial."

"If you don't want to talk about it, just say so."

"I don't want to talk about it."

She grinned. "That alone tells me a lot. Remember, I'm a detective."

"Thing is, once I tell you a heartbreak story, then you'll feel compelled to tell me one of yours. You up for that? Maybe you can give me some background on your relationships."

"Maybe," she said, "you can get right into what you've done today as my assistant."

"Thought so," I said. "See, that alone tells me a lot."

Kellie reached for her laptop and powered it up. "You have a dribble of Jell-O on your shirt. Please remove it before you give me the report."

I wiped it off. I told her about Danielle Pederson's visit to my house the night before. About Jubil's reaction. About the cross symbol found in the coffins that linked John Sebastian to the dead bodies.

Kellie listened, keyboarding it in shorthand, stopping me occasionally with questions or for clarification.

"I also went one place you didn't ask me to check," I said. "Church."

She raised an eyebrow.

"You remember Pastor Samuel," I went on. "He's been a pillar of the Charleston black community for nearly five decades. What he doesn't know, someone in his congregation will. Especially those who work for anyone south of Broad. Black servants only *seem* invisible; they hear and remember a lot. I showed Samuel the photocopy that Carmen Sebastian gave you yesterday."

"And?"

"He begged me to give up my questions. Said that more times than he cares to recollect someone in the black community has been beaten or even killed, and left behind was the very same symbol. Like a warning. Rarely gets reported to the police. And most everyone who was punished, he says, truly deserved what they got. He says it's almost like a secret police in the poor black community."

"This year? Last year?" Kellie asked. "When?"

"As far as Samuel can guess, it goes back more than a century. The news, he said, was all about the white people found under the lodge, but he says it's happened among the blacks too."

CHAPTER

11

The Citadel grounds, a sprawling campus of stone buildings that stand as proud as the boys who walk among them, lie beside the Cooper River. The cloak of Citadel tradition gives it a dignity that is palpable, and visitors feel like intruders.

I was no exception.

When the guard waved me onto the grounds, I truly felt like a stranger entering a strange land.

This was Anson Hanoway Saffron's journal entry for January 15. He would enter the Citadel less than nine months later. And so would begin the chain of events that would lead to his death.

I'm starting to read my Bible more. Mainly the beginning of the New Testament. I pretend the disciples are my friends and they have written me letters, and that's how they're telling me about their friend Jesus.

I try to imagine what it would be like to have the disciples as friends. So I've gone to the library and gotten books about the history. If people see me with the books, they'll just know I'm the loser they think I am, so I don't check the books out. I just sit in a corner and read. No one from my school ever goes there, so I'm not worried that anyone would actually see me in the library and think I was strange.

Out of all of them, I think Matthew and I would have been the closest friends.

He was a tax collector, and everyone hated tax collectors. Matthew had a little booth along the road at the end of the lake. That's where three main highways met; it was a good place to collect taxes from people going by. So Jesus went there and preached.

Matthew had his booth. When he was inside it, he was safe. Me, I just have books and I get lost inside them. And the people he didn't like, he could charge them more taxes. Me, I have to run away. Of course, when Matthew charged them more taxes, they hated him more. Which would make him hate them more back, and he would charge them more taxes again. At least that's the way I imagine it.

So there he is in his booth and maybe he hears Jesus nearby, saying all the stuff about how much God loves people. Which was really different for them to hear because they thought God was like a judge who lived in the temple. If they didn't make the right sacrifices, God would just turn his back on them. But Jesus said no, all you have to do is turn to God and he will reach out to you.

Amazing.

If Matthew and I were buddies, we would have thought that was great. Hearing Jesus say that stuff to everyone around us.

But Matthew wouldn't dare get close to Jesus, because then he would have to leave his booth where he was a representative of the government and people couldn't touch him.

So it had to be Jesus who made the first move, I'm thinking.

Maybe Jesus finally walked close by and there was Matthew, thinking this great man is going to do what everyone else does. Look away. Or spit on the ground. Or say something mean.

But in my imagination Jesus just looks at Matthew and says, "Follow me."

Matthew must have seen something in Jesus' eyes that made him get out of the booth and leave his money and the job that let him hate people from the safety of that booth.

What I'm wondering is, what did Matthew see that made him leave and follow? Something made him go against what everyone expected.

Whatever it was, it must have been good. It's something I need too.

I was at the Citadel to follow up one of Danielle Pederson's leads. James Edward Ball was a square-faced, flat-bellied man with a crew cut of salt-and-pepper hair. He wore an Adidas tracksuit and a whistle, both with obvious authority.

I stood in the bleachers of the Citadel's gym and watched him run a phys-ed class for twenty minutes, until the bell rang and his students headed for the locker room—some at a run, others at a walk. They paused occasionally to lean forward, hands on hips, and draw breath. Ball had worked them hard.

I intercepted him on the way to the locker room. "Mr. Ball," I said. "Nick Barrett." I offered him a handshake.

He was six-five and had the muscles to match his frame. He scrutinized me up and down and didn't bother to hide that he was doing it. After several moments, he reached out and squeezed my hand, much harder than necessary and much longer than necessary.

"Don't care much for civilians," he said. "And I don't have much time."

"Then I'll be blunt. What did you and Matthew Pederson have to do with the suicide of Anson Hanoway Saffron?"

We were alone in the gym. His hard stare made me acutely conscious of it.

"Go away," he said. "You've got ten seconds. Then I call security. Except I don't wait for them to get here before I make you leave myself. It won't be pleasant. You will suffer injury."

I saw in his face joy in making the threat. Saw the undisguised bully that he was. Imagined him standing over Anson Hanoway Saffron. It gave me enough anger to stand my ground.

"Ethan Osgoode. You. Matthew Pederson. Nigel Billsworth. All seniors here in '78. Someone broke the pact, Mr. Ball. I'm here because of that."

"Liar."

"Lying about the pact? Or that someone broke it?" I noticed my ten seconds had passed. And that James Edward Ball had shifted from one foot to the other. "Let me tell you a story that involves you; then you decide whether I'm lying."

I repeated the story Matthew Pederson had told his fiancée, Cheryl, all those years earlier.

✛

The four of them caught Saffron taking a shortcut from the mess hall to the dorms. Ball was at the front, not even showing a smile of satisfaction.

"Where's your salute, knob?" Ball snarled, using his height to tower above the freshman.

Saffron saluted. Too late. A mistake for a freshman, or *knob* as they were called.

"Slow, slow, slow," Ball said. "That will cost you ten push-ups." He turned to the other seniors. Osgoode. Pederson. Billsworth. "Anything else I miss?"

"Shirt not tucked in," Osgoode said, smirking. "Ten more."

"Pants not creased," Pederson added with a grin. "Another ten!"

"Egg smeared on sleeve," Billsworth said. "Twenty!"

Ball barked at Saffron. "Drop! Fifty! Now, dirtbag!"

Saffron looked past Ball and met Osgoode's eyes briefly. Osgoode kept his expression veiled.

"Drop!" Ball screamed. "Do you want sixty?"

Saffron lowered himself to his knees.

"Not here," Ball said. "There." He pointed at the edge of the grass, where cadet traffic and recent rain had left a mud puddle.

"Look at that puddle, guys," Ball said. "Must be an inch or two deep."

Saffron had not moved.

Ball grabbed him by the collar. Dragged him to the edge of the grass.

"On your hands, dirtbag," Ball ordered Saffron. "Face above that mud."

Saffron lowered himself as he was commanded. Other knobs saw him and turned quickly to avoid the possibility of getting entangled in the humiliation. When it came to hazing, few freshmen believed in solidarity.

"Count 'em off!" Ball said.

At ten, Saffron was already gasping. At twenty, each push-up took him thirty seconds, and his count was hardly more than a grunt.

"This is going to take him forever," Ball told the other three. "But stick around. It should be worth the wait."

They laughed.

At thirty-two, arms quivering, Saffron collapsed. He turned his head, but the side of his face landed solidly in the mud.

Ball knelt on Saffron's back, placing his full weight on his knees. Saffron tried to roll away from the pain, but Ball was far too heavy. Saffron's face remained partially submerged.

"Hey, little Bible-thumper," one of them said. "Shouldn't you turn the other cheek?"

The others laughed.

Ball leaned forward, dropping his face just behind Saffron's ear. "Pack your bags, boy. Go home to your mama. It's only going to get worse."

This was one of the stories that Cheryl Harper had heard from Matthew. A story plainly transcribed in the papers that Danielle Pederson had handed me the night of her visit.

James Edward Ball did not deny the event.

"Sure I helped haze Saffron," Ball said. "All the seniors did. To all the freshmen. It's how we made them tougher. It was no different when we were freshmen. The ones who survived were meant to be here."

"*Made* them tougher. As in past tense. Not *make* them tougher. The Citadel doesn't encourage hazing the way it did in the past, does it? Probably because of abuses like Saffron had to endure."

Ball shook his head. "Saffron, he deserved all he got. He was weak. Would have brought the rest of us down. We had to get him out."

Several students wandered into the gym, ready for the next class. Ball blew the whistle to get their attention.

"Far end," he barked. "Wait until I'm ready." To me, he said, "Bell rings in two minutes. I don't know who told you about Saffron, but it doesn't matter. What happened is long-ago history."

"Did the push-up incident make it to the suicide inquiry? How about the pact that the four of you seniors made?"

He flinched. I'd been looking for it.

"Or should it be reported now?" I asked. "Both what happened and how you kept it from the inquiry? Isn't that some sort of breach of ethics? Are graduates who now role-model for the students allowed to stay on when they've proven dishonorable?"

"Don't throw that word around. You know nothing about military honor."

"And you do?"

"I did what was necessary. Saffron was . . ." Ball set his jaw. Came to a moment of decision. "There was a reason he was not suited for the Citadel. Nobody but the four of us knew it then."

"And the reason?"

"None of your business. Or anyone's business. It was bad enough that he committed suicide. We weren't going to make it worse. For him or for his parents."

"But enough of a reason that the four of you decided to break him."

"Not just the four of us. We let it get around to the other seniors to put more effort than normal on Saffron. Except . . ."

The bell rang. More students trotted into the gym from the locker room.

"Except what?" I asked.

"Except he didn't break. No matter what we did."

"Not quite," I said. Quietly. "What finally happened that needed a pact of secrecy among the four of you?"

Ball placed his right hand on my left shoulder. Began to squeeze. "Mister, bringing this up again is going to smear a lot more on Saffron's reputation than it will on anyone else. I suggest you leave this alone. . . ."

The pressure grew unbearable. I reached up with my own right hand and tried to pull his wrist and hand away. The tendons of his wrist were steel cords and his arm like solid, immovable concrete.

"If you can't leave this alone, Mr. Barrett, come and talk to me somewhere not so safe for your health. I'll be happy to pick up this conversation once again."

He dropped his hand, and I was able to draw a breath.

"I hope I'm clear on this, Mr. Barrett. If I had made a pact, then honor and duty would obligate me to keep it sacred my entire life. There is nothing more for you to gain by bothering me again. And a lot for you to lose."

12

"Nicholas, you are welcome to express your utmost admiration." Glennifer made a grand, sweeping gesture at the desk in the back of the antique shop.

"I utmostly admire it," I said.

"Really? You aren't just saying that because Glennifer insisted on a compliment?" Elaine seemed as proud as Glennifer.

"Really," I said. "I don't think I've ever seen your desk so clear of papers."

"Send him on his way, Laney," Glennifer said. "This boy has the poorest manners in the South."

"Nicholas," Elaine said, "not the lack of papers. We've entered the twentieth century. Look at our telephone."

"Twenty-first century," I said. "In January of 2000, the memo went out to all the antique shops on King. We are now in the twenty-first century and—" I paused theatrically and brought my hand to my wide-open mouth in surprise. "Oh my," I said, imitating their Southern belle accents. "I declare. A push-button telephone."

"With caller ID and speaker conference button. And a Dictaphone recorder built into it. See where the cassette fits into the handset? Now Laney and I can both speak and listen at the same time. And record, if we want."

"Why the change after all these *decades*?"

"Nicholas, your manners," Glennifer said.

"Yes'm."

"In answer to your question," Elaine said, "listen to this."

She hit a button, waited, and hit a second button. Seconds later, Glennifer's voice came from the telephone speaker, followed by a male voice that I didn't recognize.

Hello?

> *Hello. Is this Glennifer Beloise?*

Indeed it is.

> *Glennifer . . . may I call you Glennifer?*

Certainly.

> *Glennifer, my name is Bob. And I'm delighted to tell you today that you are preapproved for a platinum-level credit card.*

Oh, Bob. That is so wonderful. Thanks for calling me with that great news. Please go ahead and send it to me immediately.

> *We will. I just need a few pieces of information. What is your current income level?*

Let me get you my address.

First, Glennifer, your current income level?

You silly young man, you don't need that. I'm preapproved.

You are, ma'am. It's just that—

What's the name of your company again? I'm so excited about getting a new credit card. Let me call my sister.

Ma'am, first we'll need—

Laney! Come here quick. There's a nice young man on the phone that has promised to send us a credit card. Bob, here's my sister Elaine.

Hello, Bob! That is so nice of you to give us a card. And we didn't even have to fill out any forms.

That's just it, ma'am. I will need a few pieces of information.

Glennifer, I don't understand. I thought you said this was preapproved. If it's preapproved, why would Bob be asking us for information?

I don't know, Laney. He told me it was preapproved. Didn't you, Bob? Tell Elaine what you told me. That you would send a preapproved card right away. Isn't that right, Bob?

Yes, it is. I just—

See, Laney? Give him our address. I think I hear the kettle boiling.

Ma'am! I can't give you the card unless you supply me with details of your income!

Then it's not preapproved, is it, dear? Could you call us back when it is preapproved?

Sure. Please. I need to go now.

I smiled as the phone clicked. Glennifer and Elaine shared the girlish high fives that I'd seen the day before.

"Nick," Glennifer said, "we got the phone because of telemarketers. Strangely enough, we've been plagued by them recently. We've decided we're going to record their calls. And our answers. Then put them on a CD and let other people enjoy them."

My raised eyebrows spoke loudly enough.

"Actually, all of it was Angel's idea," Elaine said. "She used the Internet and looked up ways to deal with telemarketers. She told us about the phone with a recorder in it and said it might be fun to do that. Remember how full her backpack was yesterday when she came in? Bless that girl's heart, she went out and found the new telephone and gave it to us."

"Not *gave,* Laney," Glennifer corrected. "Traded."

"She took our old rotary-dial telephone," Elaine said. "In exchange. Then showed us how to use this. Wasn't that sweet?"

"How old was your rotary dial?" I asked. If I remembered correctly, they'd had it when I was a boy, visiting the shop with my mother.

"Old enough to be an ant—" Elaine stopped herself.

I nodded. "Antique. She took it home with her last night, didn't she?"

"Antique," Glennifer said. "Humbug. A person would be lucky to get rid of that thing at a garage sale. If one stooped to that sort of activity."

"Antique," I repeated. "That explains the cell phone call I overheard Angel make this morning during breakfast. Told her friend she'd sold a funny round-dialer phone on eBay for three hundred dollars."

"Three hundred?" Glennifer came very close to yelping as she spoke. "This new phone was only eighty."

"That scalawag." Elaine's outrage was tempered by admiration. "EBay?"

"An auction system on the Internet," I answered. I rubbed my nose with the palm of my hand, trying to hide a smile. "She didn't get your old phone until yesterday afternoon. But on eBay, items are usually up for bid for at least seventy-two hours. That means she started selling that phone long before you traded it to her. Probably put it on auction a few days ago and waited until she had a confirmed bid of at least eighty dollars before she made you her offer."

Glennifer paced the short space between the wall and the desk. "This is intolerable."

"Intolerable," I agreed. "Are you going to give her the satisfaction of letting her know you're now both aware that she outfoxed you? Or should I?"

"Perhaps discretion is appropriate in this situation," Glennifer said with great dignity.

"Of course," I said. "Now let's talk about Victoria Sebastian."

✛

Barely a couple hundred yards south of the antique shop, at the corner of King and Broad, a battered yellow taxi pulled to the curb. This, like the meeting at the airport, Miles would enjoy describing to me later.

Miles had been waiting for five minutes. When the cab came to a complete stop, he opened the door to the taxi and stepped inside.

"You're on time," he said to the driver. Miles had to lean forward and speak through round holes in the center of a thick Plexiglas divider between front and back seats. "I guess that means you know to take me to the guy who sent you for me."

As the taxi accelerated back into traffic, Miles caught a glimpse of the driver's face in the rearview mirror. "Hey!"

The driver grinned. "Me. I'm the guy who sent for you. Any place in particular you'd like to go? Charleston is a beautiful city."

It was the bent old man with the red-veined nose, still wearing a John Deere cap above the same worn outfit.

"Set you up," the old man said. His voice came clearly from a speaker behind the cab's rear seat. "This isn't quite as safe as the airport, but it's not bad. We'll just drive around and talk, and when we're finished, I'll drop you off nearby, but not so close you could get in your car and follow me."

Miles leaned toward the holes in the Plexiglas again. "I don't like this. You and me, we got to be up front with each other."

The old man chuckled. "First, I'm gonna trust you about as much as you trust me. So how up front is that?"

Miles didn't answer.

"What I thought," the old man said. "Second, you don't have to talk through those holes. There's a microphone in the back. Picks up everything you say and sends it to me. Just relax and talk normal."

The old man turned onto Tradd. Traffic picked up as he

reached Waterfront. "Third, shut your cell phone off. I don't want interruptions."

Miles crossed his arms. Petulant. "Don't tell me what to do."

"There's five thousand cash in a bundle of hundreds beneath the front passenger seat. Reach under and get it. The money's yours as a down payment for future services. Now do me a favor and shut off your cell."

Miles scowled. He found the money and flipped through the bundle to make sure it was all cash, not a stack of paper like the contents of a sandwich between hundred-dollar bills.

"Wasn't expecting any calls anyway," Miles said. He reached into his suit coat and pressed the power button without pulling the cell phone loose. "So let's talk."

"No, maybe you should talk. You learning anything from the bug in the hospital room?"

"Plenty," Miles said. "And it's gonna be worth this down payment of yours."

From the other interior pocket of his suit jacket, Miles pulled out a compact disc. "What I did," he said, "was burn it onto this for you. Looks like you've got a CD player in your dash. Why don't you just play it as we drive?"

"Can't do it."

"CD player busted?"

"Works fine. Tell me, eagle-eye detective-agency man, you see anywhere in the divider a place for you to hand it to me?"

Miles didn't, of course. The divider was solid, without a little window that slid over for transactions between driver and passengers.

"So pull over," Miles said. "I went to a lot of work to get

this for you. The conversation isn't even two hours old, and I've got it on CD already."

"Nope." The old man was cheerful. "There's a reason I'm as old as I am in the facilitating business. I take zero chances. I don't even trust you enough to let you reach in my window. How about instead you give me the *Reader's Digest* version of what her friend has found out."

As the old man took them along Murray Boulevard, Miles repeated the main points, with the old man interrupting with questions. Here the taxi moved along land that had not existed a hundred years earlier. City fathers had built a seawall, then filled in behind the dyke with the dirt and rubble of buildings that had been razed by various destructions—earthquakes, fire, and hurricanes.

"See," the old man said when Miles had finished, "there's what scared my employer. She found a connection between Victoria Sebastian and the Citadel suicide. Looks like the friend's making that even more clear."

"Not much of a connection," Miles grunted. "How do you know that's why they wanted Mixson killed?"

The old man shook his head. "Don't you think I was around when Victoria Sebastian disappeared?"

Miles thought it over. Told himself not to underestimate the old man. "Then how long before they want him dead too?"

"Soon enough," the old man said. "I've got to let them know where he's been."

"Hey, if only you and I know at this point . . ."

"Foolish boy. I'm not their only source. If I hold back,

they'll wonder why I'm not telling them what they hear from elsewhere."

Again, Miles reminded himself not to underestimate the old man. Or whoever employed him.

"He's doing a good job for us," the old man said. "The longer we can keep him on the trail, the better the chances of him flushing them out. When they tell me to get rid of him, I'm going to have to stall long enough to see if he's able to make a better connection and point us where we need to go. Then we get him out of the way. Gives us a free pass to shaking down the people who wanted him dead."

"Sounds good to me, old man." Miles grinned. "When it comes to hurting him, can I do it?"

"Yes, Nick," Elaine said. "We'd heard rumors about domestic violence in the Sebastian household. We remember John's reputation as a child. Very much the bully."

"Very much." Glennifer nodded. "I believe he once put his sister in the hospital. She was eleven; he was ten. The story went out from their parents that she fell out of a tree and broke her arm. But the gossip was that John punched her and pushed her down the stairs."

The kettle at the back of their office began to whistle.

"Laney? My turn?"

Elaine nodded.

"Guest tea, please," I said. This request had become part of our daily ritual. Glennifer and Elaine, I'd discovered, had a string nailed across the inside of an old wardrobe, and they hung used tea bags inside to let them drip dry for their own private use again.

"Never dream of anything but," Glennifer called over her shoulder.

"Of course," I said. "Watching closely anyway."

I turned to Elaine. "As I said, the medical reports that Amelia reviewed showed that—"

"And how is Amelia?"

"Sounded fine," I said. If I told them she'd gotten engaged, I'd face a twenty-minute barrage of questions, some of which I wouldn't be able to answer and most that I wouldn't want to answer. "Busy as ever. She did me a big favor looking into this."

"No, Nicholas," Elaine said. "She did not. You should drop all this nonsense."

"You promised yesterday to tell me *why* I should."

"Your questions this morning over the telephone disturbed us more. Please."

"About John Sebastian . . ."

Glennifer returned with fine china and a pot of tea on a tray. Both women liked their tea strong, and I knew it would steep for another five minutes before she served it.

"John Sebastian . . . ?" I prompted.

"Well . . . ," Glennifer began.

"Yesterday I suggested that we discourage his speculations, Glennifer. Please, some discretion!"

Glennifer lifted her nose in a haughty fashion and busied herself with counting sugar cubes into the empty cups. She knew how each of us took our tea.

"John Sebastian . . . ?" I tried one more time.

"Heaven's sakes, Elaine. Tell him what we know. You can trust him to use it wisely." Glennifer turned to me. "Nicholas, do you have any idea how difficult it is for a woman in Charleston's high society to leave an abusive marriage?"

"I guess it depends on the prenuptial agreement," I said.

"If there is a prenuptial," Glennifer answered. "If money is the only consideration. Most women find it very shameful to admit that the man they married is not a source of protection and love. Moreover, with children involved, it becomes a lot messier."

"Today, I believe, it's a difficult enough thing for a woman," Elaine added. "Now, imagine how much more difficult a generation ago. And how much more difficult two and three generations ago. There were no social agencies. No prenuptial agreements to ensure a degree of financial stability if a woman left the marriage. Worse, there was a stigma. As if the woman was to blame. As if she wasn't good enough. That somehow she deserved the treatment she received."

"Where could a woman go for help?" Glennifer asked. "Especially if that woman lived in high society?"

She began to pour some tea.

"I don't like this," Elaine said. "I don't like this at all."

"We must," Glennifer said. "If you don't, I shall. Better that he hear it from us than go madly about in all directions asking others. Who knows then what might happen if the wrong people find out that he's inquiring into this matter?"

Elaine's heavy intake of breath was audible above the fan in the office. "The point we are making, Nicholas, is that without . . . shall we say . . . *help* of some sort, many women lived hopeless lives."

"Help of some sort," I repeated.

"You did not hear it from us," Elaine said. "Nor, if you ever tried to make this public, would you find any sort of confirmation."

"Secret societies, Nick," Glennifer said. "Surely in all your time at the archives you're aware that a hundred years ago secret societies were more common in Charleston than rats on the wharves."

"The Freemasons . . ."

"Perhaps," Elaine said. "Perhaps not. All we're saying is that once it appeared that a woman was in desperate need, the abusive husband would be encouraged to stop."

"In what manner?"

"I simply do not know," Elaine said. "Nor do I want to know."

"My guess," Glennifer said slowly, "is that often the wives themselves would not know who was behind it. But the abuse stopped."

"John Sebastian was beating Victoria," I said. "And, by the records, his children. To the point that one died. Then, suddenly, Victoria stopped visiting the hospital. Are you suggesting . . . ?"

Both of the elderly women nodded.

"And Whitman Metiere? The rumors about his weakness for adolescent girls?"

"You didn't hear it from us," Elaine said primly. "We're Christians. We don't engage in gossip."

"Not quite true," Glennifer said. "We listen avidly, but only to know who needs praying for."

"Remarkable," I said. "You managed to say that with a straight face."

"One hides one's weaknesses as one can," she said, smiling. "Our love of gossip is not secret, and yes, a failing."

"Glennie," Elaine said, "it's just as bad to pass along the gossip as it is to listen for it. And now you've simply encouraged Nicholas to keep looking into this."

True. I was deep in thought. If any of this were true and linked to John Sebastian, it still didn't explain Matthew Pederson's death. Unless there was something in his background that involved a Charleston girl from a high-society family. A senior cadet at the Citadel from a wealthy Miami family would certainly have his pick.

I sipped from my teacup. "Thank you," I said. And thought of the one person who could tell me if there was any truth in this.

John Sebastian.

There was enough time left in the afternoon to see him before I picked up Angel from school.

C H A P T E R

13

John Sebastian was an artist of the visual medium. Those less sophisticated in the arts—of which I was one—would have simply called him a painter. He'd won the gene-pool lottery, being born into what was rumored to be the wealthiest family in Charleston, but he'd chosen to live not in the antebellum mansion that drew the passing by of so many tourists, but farther west, in a house that overlooked Colonial Lake. Here the mansions were just as big, but the streets quieter and the property listings more exclusive.

His mansion had the large columns and wide front porch of its neighbors'. It was the very same mansion from which Victoria Sebastian had disappeared.

I stood in front of the same door where the two young Mormons had stood almost twenty-five years before. This time, of course, the door was not ajar, and I doubted that any blood spatters awaited me on the gleaming hardwood floors inside. I rang the buzzer.

"Hello?" The tinny female voice came from a speaker beside the door.

"I'm here to see John Sebastian."

"Yes? Who's calling, please?"

"I'm from the Kellie Mixson Agency."

"Oh." There was a hesitation, and the speaker crackled slightly. The woman's finger must still have been on the send button. As if she was second-guessing her decision to give the photocopied symbol to Kellie in the hospital. "Yes. I'll be right there."

Moments later the door swung open. Carmen Sebastian wore a tight red tracksuit, sleek on a body that had won her a beauty pageant twelve years earlier. Her long dark hair was pulled back, with her ponytail sticking through the back of a black ball cap. The casual look, however, was marred by the meticulous makeup job on her olive-skinned features.

"He's in his studio," she said. A set of car keys dangled from the fingers of her right hand. "Straight down the hallway. Turn right at the end, then left. Just past the bathroom. If you don't mind, I'd like you to make your own way. I'm leaving to shop for groceries now."

She gave me an apologetic smile. "Actually, I'd rather not be here when you talk to him."

The studio was essentially a large sunroom, built of arched glass onto a deck that jutted off the back side of the house. It was framed by oak trees, and scattered leaves swirled on the glass above me.

John Sebastian held a paintbrush in front of a midsize canvas. He was shirtless and in bare feet; he wore denim overalls. Victoria had been his first beauty-pageant wife when he was in his twenties; now, on number three, decades after Victoria's disappearance five years into their marriage, he was well over fifty.

I was impressed at his chest hair, sprouting obviously from his coveralls. Not impressed at the amount, of which there was a rug's worth, but at the color, which matched the jet-black hair on his head. He, like his wife, had pulled it into a ponytail. Either he was a genetic freak, or he took the time to dye his body hair too. I hoped the hair on my head kept its color like that. But I doubted I'd dye my beard.

He squared his body to me in an aggressive stance, keeping his paintbrush in his left hand. While at first glance he played the artiste role, second glance showed a dichotomy. His arm and shoulder muscles were well defined, and there was no loose flesh around his neck and chin. This was a powerful man.

"Carmen!" he called. "I have a visitor here. I was not expecting visitors!"

"Nice to meet you too," I said.

"I'm busy. If you have household matters to discuss, Carmen will be here shortly. I assume she let you in, but she has instructions to leave me undisturbed." He drew a breath. "Carmen!"

When she didn't answer immediately, he used his right

hand to lift a walkie-talkie off a nearby stool. His message was clear. I was not worth the effort of setting aside his paintbrush. He barked into the walkie-talkie, "Carmen, the studio. Now!"

I walked over to him.

His nearly completed painting was a detailed re-creation of a Civil War battle, with the outline of Charleston's St. Michael's Church looming in the background, the battle reduced to a miniature scale among the headstones of St. Michael's cemetery. Despite my inclination not to have any respect for a man who used violence against a woman half his size, I was impressed. I'd seen paintings like this in art galleries in town and had not realized they were his works. If money and pedigree had given him the leisure to pursue life as an artist, he'd certainly taken advantage of it.

He caught me taking it in and said, "You can't afford this. Now go away before I physically remove you myself."

Slowly I unfolded a piece of paper from my back pocket. Held it up in front of him and watched his eyes move over the symbol of the cross.

He pressed the button on his walkie-talkie. "Carmen, cancel that. I want to be left alone."

"Exactly," I said. "Let's talk."

He set the walkie-talkie back down on the stool. With his other hand, he placed his brush on the easel. His hand shook slightly. He drew another deep breath, but not to bark out a command. Instead he exhaled. Slowly. He leaned back against the stool, reaching behind him with both hands to brace himself, arching his chest away from me as if fleeing.

"I swear, I haven't hurt her since the last time. . . ."

I responded with a silence that built, remembering what Carmen had reported to Kellie.

"Okay, a few times I yelled some, and I might have swung, but it was nothing, really. . . ."

I continued to hold the sheet of paper in front of him, realizing to my shame that I was bullying this man.

"I hit her. I admit it. I won't touch her again. I'll go for counseling. I swear."

In this moment—witnessing such an abrupt change in attitude and body language—I tasted power. And liked it too much. I sensed briefly what it must be like for those who wielded this symbol. The cross of Christ was and is a message of humility and love—just the opposite of what this cross seemed to mean.

"Tell me what you know about this." I noticed, late, that I hadn't asked. I'd commanded. Such was corruption even around the edges of power.

"What I know about it? Then you're not from them. . . ."

That statement alone told me so much. *Not from them.*

"Tell me what you know about this."

Sebastian straightened and pushed himself away from the stool. There were only a few steps between us.

Calmly, I folded the paper and placed it back in my pocket. Given his obvious terror of the power of the symbol, I doubted he would tell me anything about it if he decided I was not behind the symbol. There was nothing to gain with more questions. And what I would lose was his promise to stop hitting his wife. If that alone resulted from this visit, perhaps the use of this power had been worth it. Even though it made me no different than those who had evidently used it before.

"Good-bye."

"Wait!" The anxiousness of uncertainty returned to his face. "Who are you?"

I had not given my name to Carmen. Nor to him. It struck me that if there truly was a group behind this symbol, it might not be wise to identify myself at this point.

"Good-bye," I repeated. "I expect I will not have to return."

I left him in his studio, staring blankly at the canvas on his easel. A man suddenly broken.

For the first time since agreeing to help Kellie, this was no longer a game. I felt soiled. And more than a little afraid myself.

C H A P T E R

14

That night, when Angel knocked on the door of my office, I closed the files I'd been reading.

"Maddie asleep?" I asked as I opened the door to Angel.

She was already in red flannel pajamas, a half hour away from her bedtime. Angel held some papers that appeared to have been printed from her computer. "With Pooh," she answered.

"Shouldn't you change her then?" I asked. This question had become part of our nightly ritual.

"No, Nick. She's asleep with Pooh the bear. Her diaper is fine." Angel rolled her eyeballs. Another part of the ritual.

"Ah," I said with great seriousness. "That is wonderful to hear. Anything else?"

"Got something for you," she said, waving the papers in her hand.

I moved down the hallway and let Angel follow. I hoped Angel would never ask why I always left the office when she knocked. But I was keenly aware that I was Angel's guardian, not her father. And just as keenly aware that we lived in a world where darker minds might speculate about why she and her sister lived in my mansion. This was one reason that Hank and Ingrid lived in the mansion as full-time housekeepers. Any time I spent alone with Angel was never behind closed doors of any room in the house, but downstairs in the television room or the kitchen. Both places were within easy earshot of the main-floor bedroom that Hank and Ingrid shared, a bedroom that also shared the wall of Angel and Maddie's bedroom.

In the kitchen, I poured milk and set out a plate of cookies. I sat at the table. Angel passed me her papers and grabbed a cookie with gusto.

I was expecting to proofread a school essay.

I was wrong.

I spent three minutes reading through the pages, then looked up. I was proud that Angel knew so much about the computer world. And more than a little afraid.

"So you want me to be a criminal too?" I asked.

"What do you mean, Nick?"

"Don't play dumb, Angel."

"Come on. It's just a little computer hacking."

"Beating someone with a stick a little is still beating someone, right?"

"That's different."

"No, it's not. What you did was wrong, Angel. And since I'm responsible for you, you put me in a bad position."

Angel stood. Carefully placed a half-eaten cookie on the plate. Pushed the plate toward me. "Good night, Nick. Starting tomorrow, I think maybe me and Maddie can stay somewhere else."

"Sit down."

Her beautiful eyes widened on her beautiful girl's face. In the time since she and Maddie had joined my household, she'd never heard that tone from me.

She sat. Placed one hand upon the other on the table. Sat with her back straight and her shoulders square.

"Listen carefully," I said. I spoke slowly, simply because I didn't know quite how to say what needed to be said. "I believe I hurt you just now. You thought you were doing me a favor. You gave me the computer printout as a gift. Am I right?"

"I'm listening, Nick."

"Am I right?"

"I'm still listening."

"I intend that we share this house for many years to come. It's highly unlikely, much as I like and respect you, that you will never hurt or upset me or that I will never hurt or upset you. It will be helpful if we can speak freely when that happens. That way the hurts and upsets can be mended. And that way you and I know that our commitment to each other will be stronger than hurt feelings."

"All right. You hurt my feelings. I was trying to help."

"I'm sorry that I hurt your feelings," I said. "That was not my intent. I am going to continue to speak to you with the respect and affection you deserve. I do not want to hurt your feelings more, but what I have to say is more important than whether you like what I say."

She stared at me, not moving.

"I'm your friend, Angel, but I'm also your guardian. When you do something that I believe needs correcting, it is my responsibility to do so. Which doesn't mean I will be perfect in my judgment, but it's the position I accepted by assuming guardianship. And it's something you need to accept along with what I offer you as guardian."

She blinked several times.

"Furthermore," I said, "it is unfair of you to threaten me the way you just did. You must know by now how much I care for you and Maddie. I know you could find a place to live, either on the streets or back in your old neighborhood. That would not be a good thing for either of you, and you know that I would do almost everything possible to prevent that. But I will not allow you to get your way by using such a threat."

I paused, hoping the softness in my voice would counter the harshness of my next words. "If you don't respect me enough to listen when I have to say things you don't want to hear, then I doubt there is anything I can do to keep you in the house. I will help you and Maddie financially until you find a more suitable guardian. Unless you want to stay. Then I expect you will never again use the threat of leaving here to try to get your way. Nor will I ever use that threat against you. And furthermore, what you did was wrong. Against the law and invasive of another person's privacy."

Angel sighed. Tried a half smile on me. "Suppose I would be a fool to take Maddie away from such a nice place to live."

I hid my own sigh. "And no one ever called you a fool."

"I'm sorry I said we'd leave, Nick."

"Thank you, Angel. Now tell me about this computer printout."

"Well," she said, "remember I found the wallet and turned it in to the lost and found?"

"I was grilled by a detective of the Charleston Police about it, but no, I don't remember."

"That sounded sarcastic, Nick. Not respectful."

I groaned. "It was. Yes, I remember Ashby's wallet. How you took it from his suit jacket while I was in the hallway with him."

"Found it," she repeated. "It had his driver's license in it. Which was mainly all that I needed."

I spread out the computer papers on the table. "That's it?" I asked. "Just his driver's license. And you got all this."

"Helped that the fool also had his Social Security number in there. Could have done some good Internet shopping with his credit card numbers, but I left them alone."

"You're a saint," I said.

"Was that sarcasm too?"

"Yes," I said. "Bad habit."

I reminded myself of her background. Reminded myself, much as I wanted to lecture her on various issues such as theft and fraud, that she and I had grown up in two different worlds. I did want her to learn, but in a way that it seemed real. By example, and that would take not only time but discipline on my part to try to be that good example.

I sighed. "Now tell me how you did it."

"Sure." She finished her cookie.

And told me the rest.

CHAPTER
15

Jack Mardell sat on the front porch of his cabin behind a scoped rifle mounted on a tripod. His gray hair looked like he clipped it himself. He wore a Hawaiian shirt that hung loose over cutoff jeans and no socks or shoes. His legs were spindly, his toenails thick and yellow. His belly was large enough to solidly support the can of beer that had not wobbled once since I'd stepped onto the porch and sat on a chair beside him.

"Only reason I agreed to this meeting," he said, looking straight ahead, "is that Jubil says you're a stand-up guy. What'd he tell you about me?"

My view was his view. The cabin was set in a clearing, a good half hour northwest of Charleston, deep in the pines and half a mile down a gravel road that funneled through the trees. At the far end of the clearing, framed by a wall of pines, sat a pile of trash as large as a bus, with a big black-and-brown mongrel nosing through it. The heaped garbage was ripe with decaying food, the smell still strong in the relatively cool air of an early autumn morning. I was grateful it wasn't a midsummer afternoon.

"Jubil said you were smart like a fox. Stubborn like a bulldog. Never gave up on a case."

Mardell grunted. He had not risen from the straight-backed chair behind the rifle as I got out of my Jeep and walked up to his cabin. Hadn't even waved or spoken a greeting. Merely stared at me from surprisingly blue eyes as I explained who I was, then waved me up beside him.

"That's what he'd say about me and my days in the department. But what'd he say about me as a retired cop?"

Given the unfinished exterior of the cabin, the height of the weeds around it, and the rust on his old pickup truck, I guessed there was no need for diplomacy.

"Said not to take it personally when you were rude and antagonistic," I answered. "Said if it was anything like his last visit out here, I should expect to find you half drunk, shooting at rats."

"Hate rats." He lifted the can of beer to his mouth, paused for a gulp. Set it down. "Hate liars. That's how I spent thirty years on the force. Chasing human rats, all of them liars. Wish I could have put a bullet in every one of them."

He grinned and reached over to shake my hand. His palm was cool and moist from the sheen on the beer can. "Jubil says you want to know about Matthew Pederson."

That wasn't the reason for my visit, but if that's what Jubil had told Mardell, I was more than willing to listen.

"He tell you where they found his body?" I said.

"Didn't have to. I still keep up on all the cases I couldn't close."

"Well . . ."

"Hang on." Mardell lifted the can of beer off his belly and set it between his legs. He leaned forward into the rifle, sighted briefly in the direction of the pile of garbage, and snapped off a shot. The loud, flat crack echoed briefly.

The mongrel scrambled forward and seconds later came up with a limp rat. He shook it, as if testing to see if it was still alive, then trotted away.

"Twenty-two," Mardell explained. Placed the can back on his belly. "Was fun before with a .357, but that didn't leave big enough pieces for the dog to enjoy. You were saying . . ."

"Jubil said you ran the investigation when Matthew Pederson disappeared."

"Nineteen seventy-eight. I was on the force eleven years when that came up. Easy to remember for a couple of reasons. First was the kid's parents. Rich. Pushy. Out-of-towners. Second was the Citadel thing. Kid was a senior cadet. One of their best in years, from all accounts. Third was the pressure to keep it low-key. This had all the earmarks of a media blowout. Rich kid disappears from military institute. And, of course, the Citadel was still dealing with the press about the other kid found dead. Another rich one. Saffron."

"They were linked," I said. "Matthew and Anson Saffron. That would have been news."

Jack's eyes opened slightly wider. "You found that out? Between the Citadel and the money behind those kids, they buried everything deep. Because that was the news they didn't want to get out. Here it is, what, twenty-five years later? And you manage to make the connection."

"Not me." I told him about Danielle Pederson. The transcribed stories from Matthew's former fiancée. I finished with a simple statement. "Danielle knew that Matthew was part of the hazing inquiry."

Jack snorted. "Part? He was a murder suspect."

It was my turn to be surprised. "I thought it was a suicide."

"What you don't know was how the kid was found. He was hanging from the basketball hoop in the gym. Attached to a cross. No one—and I mean no one—outside of a few top officials at the Citadel and some of us on the force knew that."

This is when Jack Mardell described to me the events of the night that Anson Hanoway Saffron died. How four unidentified cadets in balaclavas were seen taking him down the hallway. How he was found in the morning, with the chair turned sideways on the floor.

"Here's how it shook out," Mardell said. He had finished his beer but left the empty on his stomach. "After all our interviews, we got it down to the seniors who seemed to work Saffron over with special care. I mean, the way it worked, all the seniors hazed any freshman whenever possible. But for the most part, the hazing ended in a month. Except for Saffron. Four of them wanted him out and worked hard at it. Matthew Pederson was among those four. All of them, of course, had alibis for where they were that night. When Saffron was found dead the next morning, those four who took him had real incentive to keep their mouths shut. And since no one could identify any of the four who took Saffron from his room, we really had nowhere else to go with our investigation. That was pretty much it. We could suspect them but not prove it."

"And you believe it wasn't suicide."

"Couple of screws had been taken out of two of the wooden legs of the chair. Coincidence that they happened to take a bad chair? Or did one of the four set it up that way?"

I closed my eyes briefly, thinking about the horror. Saffron standing on the chair with the rope around his neck. Waiting for morning and rescue, even if that meant public humiliation. Hearing the first crack as one of the legs began to collapse under his weight. Feeling the slight shift as the leg began to sag. Then hearing more cracking. The chair slowly beginning to sink, then falling out from under him completely.

"Dear Lord," I said. A brief, sincere prayer. "Another case of the cross being misused to inflict terror."

"Yeah. That's why I remember. And because of one other thing." He grunted and leaned forward. "Hang on. My throat's getting dry."

Mardell left me on the porch and shuffled inside for another beer. He painfully worked his way back into his chair, then put his eye to the rifle's scope, scanning the pile of refuse for the movement of rats. Satisfied there were no immediate targets, he cracked open his fresh beer and took a long slug.

"See," he said, "we really wanted to find Matthew bad. He disappeared about the time we were just beginning to work the Saffron case hard. Everyone—other cadets—said he and some Osgoode kid were considered two leaders among the seniors, and especially that group of four. Osgoode wouldn't talk to us, and it was strange that Matthew was gone. What I heard was that he'd fallen hard for some older broad who had picked him up at a local bar. So I'm out doing grunt work, going to the places that let underage kids in, showing Matthew's photo. Sure enough, a bartender says he remembers the kid because he saw him once or twice with this real stunner, that the two of them would sit in the corner and have long, serious conversations. Didn't know who the looker was, but the kid seemed goo-goo over her. That got my attention, because we had one eyewitness lived near the Citadel say he saw a kid get into a yellow cab about the time Matthew was supposed to be in his room studying. Couldn't be positive it was Matthew, but the witness did say it looked like there was a woman in the backseat, waiting for him. And that's as far as I got. For a while."

Mardell burped. Wiped his mouth. "Fact is, I was convinced the kid had run off with her. Thought the kid had fallen for her hard. Maybe she was tired of her old man and saw someone rich to make life fun again, convinced him to take some of his family's money, run away, and live happily ever after with his new love. Made sense to me, thinking the kid's afraid of being hit with a murder rap. Really figured they'd both surface again when the honeymoon wore off."

Another slug of beer. "Then about a month after I make my rounds of the bars, that same bartender calls me back. Says he can tell me who the broad was. I say to him, 'she's been back?' I'm thinking if she's back, then finally I can catch up to the Pederson kid. Bartender says no, he just saw her photo in the paper. When he tells me who it is, I'm thinking, yeah, that makes sense. Rumor had it her husband treated her rough, so

she finds this Matthew Pederson kid. Pulls together a plan
where he leaves first and tells him to wait a month for her so
it's not obvious they skipped town together."

He had said all of that in a great rush of words and
needed a break to catch his breath. And have more beer.

I waited.

He began again. "So what I figured was this woman finds the
right time and makes it look like a murder to set up her husband,
then catches up to the Pederson kid. That's the way I had it in
my mind all along. For the next couple years, like I said, I kept
expecting one or the other of them to surface again. Now I'm off
the force, and turns out the kid never made it out of Charleston.
My question is, where'd the broad go, if not with him?"

"Who was the woman?" I asked. Although I already knew.

"The next missing-persons case thrown on my desk.
Victoria Sebastian."

CHAPTER

16

As I drove back to Charleston, I checked my cell phone for voice-mail messages. The first one was from Ingrid.

I called her after I heard the second message.

"Hello," I said. "It's Nick."

"Yes, Mr. Barrett. I thought that might be you."

"I'm not sure I understood your message. You said there was a note?"

"On the doorstep," she said. "I didn't see anyone put it there."

"Thank you. May I confirm the instructions?"

"Of course, Mr. Barrett."

"Nick."

"Nick," she said. I could hear the smile in her voice.

I confirmed. "I am to meet someone at the northeast corner of the St. Michael's cemetery at 10 A.M.?"

It was 8:30 now; that still gave me time to stop at the bank before going to the cemetery.

"Yes, indeed." Nothing in her voice betrayed any curiosity. "As I mentioned in my message, the note was signed by Isabelle Saffron."

"Thank you." I hesitated. "And did someone else call and ask for my cell number?"

"Only ten minutes ago. I hope you don't mind. This person said it was extremely urgent and extremely personal. That's why I gave it. Ordinarily . . ."

"I'm glad you did, Ingrid. It helped a lot."

"Thank you. Is that all?"

"Yes."

She hung up.

That at least solved the small mystery of how the second caller to my voice mail had known how to reach me. But it didn't tell me who it was. It didn't tell me why this person wanted to meet at noon today. Or why this person had whispered during the entire message, making it impossible to guess the identity or gender of the caller.

Most of all, it didn't explain why the caller had said the meeting would help me find Victoria Sebastian.

The small, ancient stone building of South Carolina First and its quiet, marble-floored teller area with only three teller cages hid the immensity of the assets the bank guarded for many of Charleston's fifth- and sixth-generation families. An unbroken succession of male Billsworths had been at the helm from the day it was founded late in the eighteenth century; here, behind a massive oak desk in a walnut-paneled office, Nigel Billsworth followed in the family tradition.

He was in his midforties, sleek like a well-fed seal. The pin-striped suit was Wall Street, the precise, bleached-blond haircut and pedicured nails were California, and the accent and understated but warm welcome were Charleston.

"Mr. Nicholas Barrett," he said, getting up from behind the desk, "it is indeed a pleasure. Shame about Pendleton, of course, but in the end, justice must be done."

He was referring to my half brother, who until recently had occupied the Barrett mansion near the waterfront. Now it belonged to me.

"There was a lot more to it than what made the papers," I said. Pendleton and I had come to an amiable agreement. A postcard I'd received a week ago showed he was enjoying his decision to give up all that he'd once believed important, so important he'd almost sold his soul trying to keep it. Those too were events that had resulted from my return to Charleston. "I'm sure he believes it was the right thing for him to do."

Nigel Billsworth nodded, as if he knew everything that had transpired since my return to Charleston. It was a distinct possibility. News travels among the old families as if the city were still a village.

"Please, sit." He pointed to a burnished chair that could have been in the same spot for two centuries, polished by different generations of slaves, then employees. "Coffee? Tea?"

I shook my head. "I appreciate the appointment on short notice. I know you must be very busy."

"No problem at all. Any business I could do for or with you would be wonderful. Although I'm sure you are being treated fairly at Southern Independent."

No surprise that he knew my bank. Or that he made his statement sound like a polite question. Or that perhaps the only reason he'd made my appointment a priority was the hope that I wasn't being treated fairly.

"I'm here on a different matter," I said. "Matthew Pederson and Anson Hanoway Saffron."

Billsworth's face lost all warmth.

"I see you remember those names."

"Certainly. Both are linked with tragedies that happened in my final year at the Citadel. You'll find I have very little interest in discussing either event. With you or anyone else."

The disadvantage of wearing khakis and a sweatshirt is the lack of storage space. I did not have a suit jacket like his that I could reach into for papers or a pen. Instead I had to squirm to reach into my back pocket and pull out folded sheets.

I began to read directly from the top sheet. " 'Matt and Ethan and Nigel once caught Anson on his way to class. They made him take everything out of his briefcase and explain what each item was. Anson had a fifteen-page term paper on the Citadel's role in the first stages of the Civil War. It was due that day as soon as he arrived in class. They made Anson eat the first two pages, then threw the other pages on the ground and set them on fire. They all found it funny, except Anson, who couldn't say a word of protest.' "

I lifted my eyes to meet Billsworth's horrified gaze.

"I can understand why you would remember Anson Saffron's name," I said. "Being a part of hazing and then a tragedy will do that for a person."

I held up the sheets, flipped through them so that Billsworth would see that each was filled with more to read. "The transcript of a recorded conversation with Cheryl Harper. You might remember her, too, since you were such close friends with Matt Pederson. Her maiden name was Cheryl Gibbon. She was Matt's fiancée. Seems Matt told her a lot of stories."

I flipped through the pages again. Only the top page held anything of relevance to Nigel Billsworth, but if he wanted to conclude I had reams of stories about him, that was fine with me. I filled the silence by borrowing from what Jack Mardell had told me earlier. I'd had time to think about this during my drive back from Mardell's cabin, knowing that Nigel Billsworth would otherwise have little incentive to talk to me.

"Four cadets in balaclavas took Saffron out of his dorm room the night he died," I said. "Four cadets who have never been identified. While there are witnesses to the fact that you and Matthew Pederson and Ethan Osgoode and James Edward Ball hazed Saffron on other occasions, I'm certain you never went as far as to put Saffron on a cross with a rope around his neck and taunt him to commit suicide. And because it was not you in one of those balaclavas that night, I see no need to take this written transcript any further than this office once you answer some questions for me. Because I'd hate to have the media here to ask the same questions after all these years. After all, once they've read this transcript, they might jump to the conclusion that you actually *were* part of torturing that poor young freshman. And if they were unscrupulous enough to actually run some of those stories, it'd be a shame what kind of impression that might have on some of the respectable people who are your clients."

I got up, hating the game I felt forced to play. But the stakes were high, especially since I'd found out that Saffron had not committed suicide. So a murderer—or perhaps an entire organization of murderers—might still be on the loose. I walked to his office door and shut it.

"Perhaps," I said, smiling as I returned to the expensive chair and sat again, "you would prefer that you and I have a private conversation instead."

As I watched Nigel Billsworth squirm, I thought of the chair with two screws removed. Which of the four had been the murderer?

"Ready to tell me more about the night Saffron died?" I asked.

Nigel fumbled with a desk drawer. Came up with a tall green bottle of Glenfiddich Scotch. He dropped the bottle cap on the floor as he reached for a tumbler. Didn't bother to pick up the cap. Poured and gulped half the tumbler in one shot. "I can't tell you much," he said.

"Because of the pact?"

"You know about that too?"

"Look," I said, "all I want is the truth. I'm not interested in punishing anyone for what happened a quarter century ago. With one caveat. I will not hide any kind of criminal action. If you didn't do anything criminal, tell me exactly what you did.

Otherwise, I'll assume you did and go to the media and police accordingly."

"It wasn't criminal," he said. "It was—" he stopped himself, then started again—"it was immoral, cowardly, and something the people involved should always regret. But not criminal."

"Then," I said, "it stays between us."

"I will never admit I was involved," Billsworth said. "But I can tell you about that night."

He surprised me by beginning to weep halfway through the story.

From Saffron's diary and Nigel Billsworth's story, I was finally able to piece together what had happened the last night of Anson Hanoway Saffron's life. An hour and a half before lights-out, Anson Hanoway walked down the barracks hallway to his room. Conversations slowed and stopped at his approach, then picked up again after he passed by. He told himself that it was his imagination, hearing his name occasionally spit out by his fellow cadets.

It bothered him less than it would have other freshmen. He was accustomed to a sense of apartness. Fountain pen, blue ink, spiral-bound notebook—these were the instruments of his refuge, and they awaited him in his dorm room. And so did God, his one solace besides his writing in the pressure-filled world of the Citadel. When the door was shut and he was immersed in poetry and prayer, his solitude became a blessing, not a curse.

Fifteen minutes before lights-out, Anson reread all that

he had written in the previous hour. The syllables of the words and the cadence of the sentences played like music in his thoughts. Satisfied, he slowly shut the notebook and placed it in the top drawer of his desk.

Next was his diary, which he kept in a hole he'd cut into his mattress. To get it, he removed the lower corner of his bedsheet and reached far inside the mattress.

He returned to his desk and spent ten more minutes recording the events of the day and his emotional impressions of those events.

Anson wrote quickly, without measuring each word as he did with poetry. He did this in part because he liked to give his diary the feel of stream of consciousness, as if he'd actually been recording the day's events as they happened. And he wrote with speed because he knew that his roommate would arrive in the final minute before lights-out. Soon he finished writing the day's events and moved to the bed to hide the diary again. At that moment—earlier than Anson had expected—the door to his dorm room swung open.

It was not his roommate but four cadets. Wearing black hoods.

Anson shoved the diary under the mattress, hoping they had not noticed.

The four moved toward him.

✛

"The cross was Ethan's idea," Nigel said. He caught himself. "At least, that's what I heard. Because outside of this room,

I will deny to my dying breath that I was one of those four. And you would have no way of proving it."

"Of course," I said. If these were the ground rules, I was happy with them. For now.

"Saffron was standing up to all the other hazing," he said, speaking slowly. He dabbed at his face with a handkerchief. "It was getting to the point where Matthew and I and some of the other senior cadets were actually beginning to admire Saffron. His faith and all he stood for. Not Ethan. He hated Saffron. It was almost unnatural."

"Any idea why?"

"None. I think it was in the diary."

"How did you know about the diary?"

"Matthew picked it up." Nigel grimaced, realizing he'd made another mistake. "So I heard."

"So you heard."

"As Anson fought, we—those four who were there, I mean—threw him on his bed to tie him down. The mattress moved. The diary hit the ground. Ethan tried to grab it, and Matthew beat him to it. But Matthew never gave anybody a chance to read it. I think that's why he and Ethan got into a fistfight a few days later. Ethan wanted it as badly as I'd seen anyone want something, as badly as he wanted Saffron to quit the Citadel."

"Nothing worked until the cross?"

Nigel nodded. "Anson surprised everyone with how tough he was. Looking back, I think Ethan thought Saffron would be an easy target among the entire freshman class. When Saffron didn't fold in September—the way he suffered in silence and took all our hazing—it just made Ethan angrier and angrier. And from October on, it got worse and worse for Saffron. Until . . ."

"He was up on the cross and decided to kick the chair over," I said.

I watched Billsworth closely. Did he know that two of the screws had been taken out of the legs of the chair? That it hadn't been a suicide?

"That shocked me," Billsworth said. "Really. What I heard . . ."

"Because, of course, you weren't there. . . ."

"Exactly. What I heard was that Matthew said that this would be the last time anything was done to Saffron. If Saffron didn't quit, he would put word out to the seniors to leave him alone. None of us expected that Saffron would actually kill himself. He was just so calm about all the other times we hazed him. Dignified. Like he was almost sad for us. In a way, it didn't make sense with what Ethan had told us about him."

"Told you what?"

"That I can't answer."

"The pact."

"That I can't answer."

Which was answer enough.

I was beginning to feel sympathetic toward Billsworth. My guess was that he'd gotten caught up in the hazing of Anson Saffron, without realizing as a teenager what it was like to be on the wrong side of that kind of persecution.

"Weird thing is," Billsworth said, "the next week, I heard that Matthew had decided to become one himself."

"One what?" I asked.

174

"A believer. Like Anson Saffron."

I thought about that and compared it to what I already knew about Pederson. "But Pederson didn't mind going to bars with a married woman," I said.

Billsworth held the bottle over his tumbler, then set it down without pouring.

"What don't you know about all of that?"

Billsworth just stared at me.

I stared back.

Billsworth hesitated, then finally said, "She wasn't married. Or at least Matt didn't know if she was. He said she was his soul mate. Could pour out all his troubles to her. We asked about his fiancée, and he said it was over. We said we wanted to meet this mystery woman, and he said when the time was right."

"You think he ran away with her?"

Billsworth began to pour himself more scotch. "I try not to think about it. Really. I'm very ashamed of what happened. You can punish me by spreading the story you just read to me, but trust me, I've already punished myself. A lot of sleepless nights."

"I've had a lot of sleepless nights of my own," I said, standing. "You want to talk? Call me anytime." I handed him my card.

"Yeah," he said. He studied the glass. "That's it? We're done?"

"One last favor," I said. "Any idea where I can find Ethan Osgoode?"

"That you don't know, huh?"

I waited.

"Killed in a car accident. About a month after Saffron committed suicide. Was in his car at a stop sign, and a semi rear-ended him. Spun him out into traffic and about three other cars broadsided him. He didn't have a chance."

C H A P T E R

17

I walked among the dead of St. Michael's.

St. Michael's Church was at the corner of Broad and Meeting Streets. As the first Episcopalian church in North America, it had a venerable history. Some of the signers of the Declaration of Independence were buried here, and many of the parishioners took their glory from the esteemed dead.

I was familiar with the grounds. I visited it every week. My own son, stillborn, was buried here. I would visit his grave and mourn the loss and reflect on the circumstances that had led me away from him, then back to Charleston years after my marriage had been annulled.

I could never leave the church grounds without a sense of sadness and peace and gratitude for the awareness of the power of God's presence. Here, in front of my son's headstone, I could not breathe without being reminded of how fleeting each breath was, and in turn, how fleeting this life. Without God, life was dust that had no meaning. With God, hope transformed life and its sorrows. I had discovered that hope, and the love and forgiveness of God too, after a long struggle. And I had learned that these ancient truths of the soul are undiminished by the passage of countless generations.

I had been on the grounds in fog, in rain, in sunshine. Today, low clouds covered the sky, and a breeze with a hint of bitterness plucked at the early leaves that had fallen.

It was ten o'clock. I'd just left the bank for here.

I found the sender of the note where she had promised.

At the time she had promised in the note.

In the northeast corner, near the headstone that marked where Anson Hanoway Saffron was buried.

At the far corner, near the iron fence that separated the grounds from the street behind, stood a large man in an overcoat. As he watched us carefully, I guessed he was Isabelle Hanoway Saffron's caretaker.

She sat hunched in a wheelchair in front of the headstone. She'd wrapped herself in a dark shawl, with only unadorned fingers showing where they gripped the edges. Age had thinned her face and speckled it with moles. The feathers of her hat fluttered in the breeze.

"You are Nicholas Barrett," she said in greeting.

"I am." Conscious of my height while she was seated, I knelt beside her.

"I understand you have been asking questions about my

son." She remained as she had been on my approach, staring at the headstone.

ANSON HANOWAY SAFFRON.
May 12, 1961–March 3, 1978.
In the arms of his Savior for all time.

"I have," I answered. Remarkable that she knew already. It had only been the day before that I had visited James Edward Ball.

"And have you considered whether my family's tragedy is truly any business of yours?"

"I have," I answered.

"And still you persist?"

"Mrs. Saffron, another woman lost her son too. A son who knew your son. She wants to know how and why her own son died."

"After all these years?"

"I have a son buried here too," I said. "Time only softens the grief. It doesn't change the sense of loss. Only God can do that."

"I am asking you to stop with your questions." Finally she turned her head to look directly into my eyes. The skin of her face sagged, and her eyes were a pale, bleary blue. "Surely we can leave the past in the past. Anson did not deserve what happened to him then. He doesn't deserve to be brought into whatever you are bringing to light now."

"I understand," I said. "I will tell this woman how you feel." Life burst into the old woman's face. She pointed at me, still clutching the shawl. "You, young man, have no idea how I feel!"

It was a well-deserved rebuke.

"No," I said quietly. "I don't."

"Let me tell you about Anson," she said. "He is not a piece in some puzzle you are trying to put together. He was flesh and blood. *My* flesh and blood."

✢

Just before his fifth birthday, it was discovered that Anson Hanoway Saffron had leukemia. Isabelle believed he was being punished for her sins—the excessiveness of lifestyle that she enjoyed as a wealthy woman—so she converted to Christianity and pledged Anson's life to God if he would spare the boy.

The doctors called it a miracle cure, because within six months, they could not discover any sign of the disease.

Isabelle remained true to her pledge. She began attending church regularly. While her husband refused to go, she took Anson each Sunday, reminding him that his life was special and had been dedicated to God. Anson seemed to care little.

Until, years and years later, at age fifteen, his inward searching for meaning and truth led him to become a Christian. Shortly afterward, he read about leper colonies and decided that he wanted to serve God by serving those people. His father hoped this foolish, childish dream would pass, but Anson started to talk about dropping out of school as soon as he turned sixteen to fulfill his destiny.

Isabelle had been amazed at how Anson had stood up to his father. So she had stepped in and negotiated a deal. If Anson graduated from the Citadel, the family would finance the mission of his choice. His father agreed, believing that the Citadel would toughen up his son, making him lose his idealistic bent.

So it was that Anson Hanoway Saffron entered the Citadel in the fall of his sixteenth year.

"When Anson died in the manner that he did," Isabelle finished, "my deal with God was over. I didn't stop believing in God. I simply saw no reason to ever follow him again. He wasn't my enemy nor was I his. I just wanted nothing to do with him ever again." She smiled grimly. "It is a vow that I have kept. I am not far from death myself, and not even with that prospect can God bully me into turning toward him again. My loss is too great."

I could think of nothing to say at first. A full minute passed. The breeze gusted into a wind, and sparrows fought on the ground near us among the scattering wisps of fallen palmetto leaves, long dried by sun and wind.

"I know something about loss too," I said at last, quietly, meeting her eyes. "I did not know my father. My mother was taken from me when I was ten years old. My own son, stillborn, was buried in this cemetery before I knew he existed. And yet I returned to God." I paused. "Maybe you will too."

"I am old. I have no time for your platitudes."

"Maybe not. But we have time to help another mother find the truth about her son."

"You aren't going to leave this alone, are you?" she said.

"I cannot."

"Then do this for this old mother," she said. "Find out why they did what they did to my Anson."

She motioned for the large man in the overcoat. He ignored me as he came over and wheeled her away.

I stood alone in front of Anson's headstone for several more minutes as the husks of broken palmetto leaves swirled over my shoes.

C H A P T E R

18

"This is what I want to know," Jubil said over the cell phone. "How did you get that stuff on Ashby?"

"Is it true?"

"I hate it when you answer a question with a question. If a perp tried it on me, I'd be on his throat like a Rottweiler. Let me repeat. How'd you get that stuff on Ashby?"

"Perp?" I said, walking down King Street toward the antique shop. Sunlight played off the ancient stone of the older buildings. "Is that cop talk?"

"There you go with the questions again. See, some of what you gave me on Ashby, I'm not sure I could get myself without a warrant."

"Is it true?"

"You're tiresome."

"So it is true." I stepped aside to make room for a mother holding hands with a determined toddler.

"Yes. Foster homes. Juvie records. Time in a state pen. Even the therapy sessions. Except all I could get on that was that he'd made appointments with a shrink while he was in the pen—nothing about what they talked about. Happy? Now where did you get it?"

"Internet," I said. "Amazing the stuff you can find if you know where to look."

"Nick . . ." His voice held dark warning, audible even through a cell phone connection.

"Jubil, if any laws were broken, I promise it won't happen again."

"*Were* broken? Nick—"

"Got to go. Buy you breakfast sometime."

"Nick—"

I hung up. And walked into the antique shop owned by my friends.

✦

"Nicholas Barrett, look at this!" Glennifer waved some papers at me. I'd barely stepped through the doorway to their office.

"Well," I said, smiling, "good morning to you too."

"It's *your* Angel," Elaine said. "You should see what she wants to make off us."

"*My* Angel, huh. Not *our* Angel? What is it? An offer for any of your rotary-dial telephones from home?"

"Not amusing, Nicholas," Glennifer said. "Not at all. Look at this, please."

I accepted the sheets of paper. "May I sit?"

My prosthesis felt like it was cutting into my leg. It seemed like I had walked more than usual already.

"Certainly." This from Elaine.

"And tea?" I asked.

"Certainly," Glennifer said with some impatience. "Please read it and tell us what you think."

I finished scanning the papers before the kettle began to whistle. Angel had put together a professional-looking proposal. Essentially, it was an offer to set up a Web site exhibiting their current inventory of antique furniture. She would maintain and update it as necessary, and handle the sales and shipping.

"I don't think it's a bad idea," I said.

"I beg your pardon?" Glennifer said. "Did you see the hourly rate she wants?"

"About half of what you'd be charged by anyone else," I said. "And she's as good as you could find, twelve or not."

"She wants 15 percent of sales," Elaine said. "Did you read that part?"

"Knowing Angel, I expect she's very willing to settle for 10. After all, more than once she's been in this very office listening to you two shrewdly negotiate with a hapless client." I set the papers on the desk. "Seems to me that you don't have much to lose. She's put a cap on what it will cost you to set up the site. I'm guessing she figures to get her reward on the back end if the idea works."

"Either way," Glennifer said, "that's a lot of money for a twelve-year-old. When I was her age . . ."

"You had a family," I said.

I let them ponder that before I continued. "Sounds like when you read the proposal, you felt she was trying to make money off you. I see a girl who is determined to take care of her little sister. I've noticed Angel saves every penny she gets."

"They have a guardian," Elaine said. "You. And it doesn't look like you'll go broke soon."

"Angel lost her mother and her grandmother. Think she ever wonders if I'll be taken away too?" I'd lost my own mother when I was young. I didn't have to search my soul too deeply to understand Angel's fears.

"Oh." Glennifer put an arm around Elaine. "That makes me so sad. Perhaps we should hire her for the Web site then."

"Not for that reason," I said. "She'd be humiliated if she ever thought you agreed to her proposal out of pity."

"He's right," Elaine said. "We'll consider it on the merits alone."

I waited as Glennifer readied our tea. This daily ritual with these two dear and quirky ladies had become important in my life. I was grateful for it.

"Two questions," I announced. "First one is this. Any more telemarketing calls?"

The broad grin on Elaine's face made the question worthwhile. "Nicholas! Listen to this."

She fiddled with the cassette until a taped conversation began. It was marked by the typical few seconds of silence while the telemarketing computer registers that a phone line has been answered. Then came a male telemarketer's voice, with Elaine's following.

Hi. My name is Michael. I'm with—

Gord! Don't try to tease me like that. I'd never forget your voice.

Ma'am? Actually, I am Michael. I'm with—

Still the same silly sense of humor, Gord. I miss that. Do you really think after five years of marriage, I'd forget?

There's this program I'd like to explain. It can save—

Gord, the kids are teenagers now. But they really miss you. Every day I tell them that Daddy loves them. You do love them, don't you?

Once again, I must tell you. My name is—

My father's dead now, Gord. So you don't have to worry about him hauling out that shotgun again. And I've forgiven you. Shouldn't you come home now?

I'm not—

Then why did you call? This is breaking my heart, Gord. Don't tell me you're still with that floozy? What that horse-faced old nag has that I don't is beyond me.

Ma'am—

Tell me! Is it her? My father might have passed on, but I didn't bury his shotgun with him. Where are you living? I'm going to reverse trace this call and come find you.

I'm not Gord!

I'm so sorry for yelling at you, sweetheart. Just give

*us one more chance, all right? I'll even start to shave my
legs if you come back—*

Click.

Gord? Gord?

Glennifer and Elaine giggled as the tape ended.

I applauded from my chair. "Couple more like that, and
you can compile a best-seller."

"It's certainly more lighthearted than the subject you're
going to bring up with your next question." Glennifer leaned
forward to refill my china cup. "Because I can predict what it will
be. That tawdry suicide affair. I do wish you'd give this up, you
know."

Glennifer's tone of voice had become more serious, and
I looked up sharply from the spoon of sugar that held my
attention.

"Yes, Nicholas, there's an eerie coincidence here, except
I doubt it's coincidence."

"Oh?"

"Yesterday you asked if I could find out anything about
the suicide of Anson's grandfather."

I nodded. I had asked just before leaving the shop.

She continued. "I made a couple of phone calls to old
friends. It didn't take me long to learn far more than I wanted."

"Thank you."

"I don't want thanks. Truly. This entire matter disturbs
me. After all, Whitman Metiere's body was discovered under
the lodge, was it not?"

It was. So far, the only body publicly acknowledged by the Charleston Police Department.

"And didn't you tell us under the strictest confidence about that young man Matthew Pederson? That he was involved with the hazing that led to Anson Saffron's suicide?"

Again, I nodded.

"Here's what I don't like, Nicholas." Glennifer spoke softly. "It was Whitman Metiere who forced Anson's grandfather to the point of desperation. Jesse Hanoway owned a business that owed Whitman Metiere a great deal of money. Metiere forced the banks to begin foreclosure proceedings on the Hanoway family."

"But earlier," I said, "you told me that Metiere loaned Hanoway enough money to help him retain his business."

"I did tell you that. Because he did. What I didn't know was the behind-the-scenes happenings, how Metiere pushed Hanoway to the edge. Nobody knows exactly what he did. Or why. But Hanoway hanged himself in Metiere's garage, you know. He had a note in his pocket that said Metiere was responsible for all his family's ruin."

"Even though Metiere had loaned them money to save the business from foreclosure proceedings that Metiere himself initiated?"

Both Glennifer and Elaine nodded.

"Strange, isn't it, Nick?" Glennifer said.

"It seems to me," Elaine said, "that Metiere was a cruel man."

"Let me be sure I follow," I said. "Isabelle Hanoway is Jesse Hanoway's daughter. She married into the Saffron family.

It was her son Anson who was found dead at the Citadel. He, like his grandfather, was found dead at the end of a rope."

I didn't add that it had been murder. Or that Anson was further linked to his grandfather by the fact that Matthew Pederson's body was found in the same place that his grandfather's business associate had been found.

"Essentially that is it," Elaine said. "There are some, then, who might say that by the way he died, Whitman Metiere reaped what he had sown during a long, hateful lifetime."

CHAPTER

19

For the second time that day, I accepted an invitation to St. Michael's Church. But not the cemetery—instead, the sanctuary.

I began my wait as I'd been directed in the voice mail. The sanctuary's lighting was subdued, the silence loud. Although my conscious mind assured me that I was safe, primal fear prickled at the nape of my neck. I sat sideways in a pew, determined that the person who'd sent the message would not catch me unawares.

The cross at the front of the church held my attention. What a symbol of peace and hope, that God would reach down to man and die on it as the ultimate sacrifice for the sins that would otherwise make the chasm between us and God infinitely deep and wide. Yet how often had it been abused and misused over the centuries, so that those who were truly broken and in desperate need of that peace and hope viewed the same cross with suspicion and fear.

Each time the church doors at the back swung open, throwing a wide beam of light down the aisle, I squinted to try to make sense of the outline of the person entering. Three times tourists walked in and spoke in hushed awe at the back of the church.

The fourth visitor, however, slowly walked up the aisle. She was large and old, wearing sunglasses. Her hair was long and unkempt, a dirty blonde. She wore an overcoat, with the hem of a dark dress down to her ankles, and my sense was that she shopped for clothing at a thrift store. As she moved closer on wide-heeled shoes, I was able to see her face in the light from the windows. I saw that the plainness extended to square jaws and square cheekbones beneath the sunglasses. In a parody of womanhood, her face was garishly painted with far too much makeup, put on far too sloppily.

She stopped at my pew and slid in beside me. I edged away, wary of an attack, then felt ridiculous because of it. Cheap perfume overwhelmed me.

"Promise first that we'll leave separately." Her voice was a low, manly rumble. Strangely familiar.

I nodded. This woman would not be my first choice of companions anyway.

"Lean forward, as if we are a couple, praying."

Then it clicked. The strangely familiar male voice from this ugly woman. "John Sebastian," I said.

"Lean forward. Please."

I did.

"Secret life?" I asked.

"This is nothing I would do if I didn't have to." He spoke tersely. "I can't be seen with you. And you may be watched. Anytime. All the time. I don't know."

His fear was palpable. And slightly contagious. I fought the urge to look around.

"When you came to visit," he said, "I knew who you were. I was afraid to let you know, in case it made you come back. But I thought about it after. You know nothing about that detestable symbol you showed me. You're looking for them, aren't you?"

"Them?" Although I knew who he meant.

"Don't play games with me. This is not a game. I'm terrified of them. So was Victoria. She couldn't live with the fear. Neither could I, but I wasn't prepared to give up everything I had here in Charleston. She was."

"Are you saying . . . ?"

"I'm saying I'd done some things wrong in our marriage. No, I won't lie. I'd done some horrible things. I'd made that marriage a torment for her. Then came the night I paid the price. When I tell you, you'll understand why I'm so afraid now."

Sebastian turned his face toward me. It was the first time our eyes had met since he'd walked into the church. I saw desperation.

"I want you to know what it was like. If you repeat this to anyone, I'll deny it. If you repeat this to anyone, it will probably happen to you. They are real."

✜

The ceremony happened on the night of the All Saints' Ball; Metiere's descendants had been only too happy to carry on the tradition despite his disappearance at the event decades earlier.

It took place in a carriage house in Charleston that had once been used as slave quarters. For decades after the last of the slaves had been declared free, the small building beside the Metiere mansion's beautiful garden had housed the aristocracy's other beasts of burden. As a result, the interior still smelled faintly of the horse sweat and hay dust that had replaced the earlier odors of human fear and humiliation and suppressed rage.

Where straw had once been used for the slaves' beds and later for the horses' stalls, there was now merely dirt. The interior was a shell, not yet converted to a cottage in the manner of other similar carriage houses behind other mansions. Black sheets covered tiny windows, and on this evening they blocked the glow from the orange full moon that hung just above the nearby mansion.

Those same black sheets hid from the outside the light of candles burning on an elaborate wrought-iron stand. This was the light that cast a circle, with the shadows beyond complete darkness.

Thirteen cloaked and hooded figures gathered at the edges of the flickering light, surrounding an open coffin on the dirt floor.

The coffin was not empty.

From the mansion across the garden came strains of gaily played orchestra music, but it was not loud enough to mask the groans of the man wedged inside the coffin, staring upward at the thirteen figures.

John Sebastian. Now without the joker's mask he'd worn to the masquerade ball.

He was bound at the ankles and wrists. A gag had been tied so tightly around his mouth that it cut into his lips and tongue like the steel of a horse's bit. His nostrils flared with terror and with the effort of breathing. His puny efforts to kick free of his bonds had nearly exhausted him.

One of the thirteen stepped forward from the circle and knelt at the head of the coffin. "Lift your hands."

The words reached Sebastian as a gentle whisper. A chilling whisper, because it implied such complete power that there was no need to try to frighten him more. A chilling whisper, because in his confused fear, Sebastian was forced to strain to hear every word, to involve all his senses in the ceremony.

"Lift your hands," the whisperer repeated.

Sebastian did. Slowly. Uncertainly.

The kneeling figure stretched an arm, placing an object in the man's hands. The light of the candles showed a cross of medieval design, as long and as wide as one of the man's palms.

Believing this meant he would be killed soon, Sebastian groaned again and struggled frantically at his bonds.

The one who knelt nearby reached out and pinched Sebastian's nostrils shut until he stopped movement.

"Good," came the whisper. "Listen to us, and we will let you breathe. Fight, and you will not breathe. Nod to let me know you understand."

The other twelve figures stared down on him. Silent. Unmoving. Nearly invisible against the black background.

Sebastian nodded. When his nostrils were released, he sucked in air so hard that it made a small whistling sound.

"We know the evil you have committed against your wife and children," the voice at his ear said. "Do you deny it?"

After a slight hesitation, Sebastian shook his head.

"You accept that you are guilty?"

Sebastian nodded.

"Then confess your guilt. And promise that you will never commit this evil again."

Sebastian nodded.

"Will you do this now?"

Sebastian nodded.

The figure stood and waited until the man made his promise. Then the figure continued in the same gentle whisper. "Tonight you will not die. But this is a taste of how you will die if you commit your evils again. For if you harm another woman or child, we will know. We will return. On that night, the lid will be closed upon you. And on that night, unlike this night, it will be sealed forever."

At those words the figure began to close the lid of the coffin. Sebastian's eyes bulged with renewed terror; then he was lost in complete darkness as the lid cut him off from the candlelight. He gasped for air, breathing shallowly and quickly in the absolute fear of his confinement. With hands and feet bound, he kicked and thumped against the coffin. The sounds would have been plainly heard to anyone standing nearby.

But as the orchestra music continued to float across the warm evening air outside the carriage house, John Sebastian screamed silently into his gag, believing he'd been left to die a horrible death.

"Her perfume was on one of the men," John told me when he finished describing what had happened to him. His large hands were on his knees, paint-splattered fingers splayed across the material of his overcoat. "It was an expensive perfume, very distinctive. When I was in the coffin, one of them leaned over me, and I smelled her all over him, like she'd found a way to be with him during the All Saints' Ball. I never dared ask her about it. But it's always haunted me. Did she begin the affair because she loved him, then discovered he was part of this group? Or did she somehow find out he was part of the group and begin the affair to get his help?"

I could not answer that, of course.

"I tell myself that I was spared because of it. That she forced him to come back and set me free. Because just before dawn, the coffin was opened again. The man ran before I could get out. But again, I smelled her perfume on him. Our marriage was a sham from that night on. But I never hurt her again. Or Sophia. I began to believe I was safe. When Victoria told me she wanted out, I thought she meant a divorce. But she wanted to run away from them. From me. So I helped make it happen."

"Her disappearance?"

"Not difficult. Early that morning, she cut her fingers, threw blood everywhere."

He paused, and his eyes stared beyond me. "That's the worst of my memories. How she coldly and deliberately sliced those fingers. That's how badly she wanted to get away from me."

I didn't interrupt his silence.

He drew a deep breath and composed himself. "She broke some lamps, made it look like there had been violence. She bundled little Sophia into our car, and I took her to the train station in Greenville, about two hours away. I drove back to Charleston, then resumed my normal activities. Back then, my studio was not at the house. When the police called, I acted surprised about all of it. . . ."

"But if you were warned never to hurt her again, weren't you afraid they would punish you as they'd promised?"

"Victoria said she would take care of it. I didn't hear from them. Except the once. Carmen . . . I'd lost my temper a few times and . . ."

I nearly felt sorry for him. Reminded myself that he'd probably killed his own son in an act of violence. That, even as he was admitting the punishment delivered, he was carefully hiding the crime. "I don't understand," I said. "Why tell me now? Why go to all these lengths to meet and—"

"I want them found," he said. "I will live the rest of my life in fear unless you can expose them."

"If you have no idea—"

"She knows," John said, with a mixture of savageness and fear. "Find her. You said you were looking for Victoria. Find her. She knows."

I asked the obvious question. "Where should I look?"

198

C H A P T E R

20

Just under two hours later, I boarded a Canadair 3000 jet at Gate 23 of the Charleston International Airport. I'd checked in with no luggage and no carry-on. That, plus the facts that my ticket purchase was a walk up and that I'd made the flight just before the cutoff, made me a prime target for security searches.

I didn't mind. Anything anyone does to make flying safer is fine with me. I did not like to fly. I am among those in the camp who fervently hold that even though I believe in Jesus and know I'm going to heaven when I die, I have no desire to get there any faster.

Preflight was a time for me to turn my head away from the crowd moving up that aisle and pray, grateful that my soul was in God's hands.

After my prayer, I stared out the window at the tarmac, feeling my stomach muscles quiver with the fear I had of flying.

It did not help to know that after I landed in Atlanta, I'd board another jet and fly again.

Destination?

Las Vegas.

✛

There was no doubt that Matthew Pederson was linked to Victoria Sebastian. And if Jack Mardell was correct, Victoria had been one of the last people to see Matt alive. If I could find her, not only would I have helped Kellie with her case, I'd be one step closer to finding out for Danielle Pederson why and how her son had died.

I was grateful for an uncrowded flight from Atlanta to Vegas. I took an emergency-exit-row seat by a window. The middle seat beside me was open. During the flight, I had intended to distract myself from my fear of flying by immersing myself in a mystery thriller, but I couldn't get hooked. Not with the questions swarming through my brain.

If lodge members were behind the deaths of the men found in the caskets, what was the link to Matthew Pederson? What had Matthew and the three other cadets done that needed a secret pact? What was Victoria Sebastian's involvement in this? And lastly, who had sent Kellie looking for Victoria?

If John Sebastian was right about the place to find her, perhaps I'd find the beginning to those answers.

But I didn't expect it to be easy.

Because of the three-hour time difference, I was in my rental car and driving away from Las Vegas by six o'clock local time that evening. My body clock, however, said it was nine, and that, combined with the time I'd spent sharing pressurized air with three hundred other passengers, left me more than tired.

According to the map, it looked like I still had about an hour's drive ahead of me. I drove south, up through the mountains south and east of Las Vegas. The city lights filled the valley, neons of man-made glory that still paled in comparison to the stars against the black of night ahead of me.

My academic background was in astronomy, but I'm not prepared to say that made me appreciate the grandeur of the sky any more than those stargazers who are ignorant of the nuclear fusion that makes the light possible. The irony is, after I'd learned everything I could in modern astronomy, I'd gone full circle, joining the ancients when they declared that in the skies was the face of God. I was fond of the first few verses of Psalm 19: *"The heavens tell of the glory of God. The skies display his marvelous craftsmanship. Day after day they continue to speak; night after night they make him known. They speak without a sound or a word; their voice is silent in the skies; yet their message has gone out to all the earth, and their words to all the world."*

I rolled down my window to let the night air pour across me. Down on the other side of the mountains, the highway was reduced to two lanes, and within minutes the traffic dwindled as I began to cross another long, wide desert valley.

201

When the road began to climb again, nearly forty-five minutes later, I had almost reached my next destination.

Searchlight, Nevada. Former mining town, then ghost town, Searchlight was now a stop with gas stations, a few restaurants, and of course, a couple of casinos.

John Sebastian had told me that four or five years after Victoria's disappearance from Charleston, a fellow country-club member had called him from Lake Havasu City, Arizona, two hours' drive south of Searchlight. The member insisted he'd seen Victoria, or at least a dead ringer, then apologized for using the phrase *dead ringer,* in case it hadn't actually been Victoria.

John had said thanks and promised to look into it. A few days later, he had called the member and reported that it wasn't Victoria, but someone who did indeed look very similar. And that's where John had left it.

Until I'd walked into his life with the cross symbol.

It would have been easy to believe that the Star-Spangled Restaurant had been at its location since the 1960s. On my right as I walked through the entrance was a state map tacked to the wall. Pencil and ink scribbles of various hues showed that it had been marked over the last few decades.

The place smelled of old grease, and the tables and sit-down counter had Formica tops. There were, of course, the ubiquitous slot machines. Although the tables and counter were empty of customers, all five slots were being used.

At the counter, I ordered coffee from a dark-haired girl. Her once-white uniform was as wrinkled as a bulldog's face, and her lack of smile matched.

"I'm looking for Tammy," I told the waitress. "I spoke with her earlier today."

"That's me."

"I'm—"

"You're the guy who called looking for someone. I recognize you from your *Gone-With-the-Wind* way of talking."

"I'm the guy." I said nothing about how little enthusiasm anyone had shown in helping me when I called just after speaking with John Sebastian. "You remember, then, that I was hoping to fax you a photo."

She shook her head, disgusted at my stupidity. "And you remember I told you we didn't have a fax machine here."

"Yes," I said as patiently as I could. "That's why I'm here. To show you that photo."

"Where you from again?"

"Charleston."

"I'm not good with knowing where my states are. That's far away, right?"

"By the Atlantic."

"Oh," she said, "close to California. I'm going to the ocean sometime, I keep telling myself. Is it nice?"

I nodded. "Is it okay now? To show you the photo?"

"This is a long ways to drive just to show me a photo. You got ahold of me at the beginning of my shift, and here you are already. You must want to find this woman bad. What was her name again?"

"Victoria Sebastian."

The only way that a girl this young would recognize Victoria Sebastian was if Victoria still lived and worked here. It was a long shot. I'd hoped to find a manager or owner, someone with some continuity.

I showed her the picture. A head-and-shoulders shot that Kellie had in her files.

"Don't remember working with her. 'Course, I only been here a couple months. You ought to see Sally Morrison. Only don't call her that. She wants to go by Marcella. It was her showgirl name. Imagine that, someone that old still thinking of herself as a showgirl. You ask me, I think she was the opening act the night Vegas first opened. You know, with Bugsy Siegel and them. You ever see that movie? About how Vegas got started?"

I plunked down five dollars for my coffee. "Where can I find Marcella?"

"She lives in a double-wide. About once a day she tells me how some guy gave her the property and the double-wide as a tip. See, he drove into Vegas from Searchlight every weekend, and on a Saturday night once he won big in the slots, and she was serving him drinks. He told her he was tired of this town, and he was moving somewhere else, and she was welcome to the double-wide. Me, I'd have taken twenty bucks, someone gave me the choice. 'Course, even this place is starting to grow now. So her property's worth something after all."

Tammy eyed me as she dug around for change, making it an elaborate act of difficulty.

"That's fine," I said. I put down another five. "Here. It's not twenty bucks, but it's not a double-wide."

"You're funny," she said. "You know that?"

"Can you tell me how to find it?"

"Sure. That's worth twenty bucks. First left, two streets, then a right and then another left up the hill."

"Thanks."

I reached the door and her voice stopped me. "Mister."

I turned.

"You look like a good guy. I'll give you some advice. No charge."

"Sure."

"If you're going to visit Sally, take a big bag of cat food."

On the flight to Nevada, I'd thought of my own death. Simply because I was in the air, five miles above the ground, in a vehicle constructed of a couple hundred tons of steel, one that from that height would have the landing capacity of a piano if the jet engines ever lost power.

Death. What did life matter if death was the only end to it? I was not the first, of course, to consider this question. Nor would I be the last.

Anson Hanoway Saffron, too, frequently thought of death and recorded those thoughts in various passages. Even though it was the writing of a fifteen-year-old, I could see the progression of his growth into faith—a faith that was not "just his parents' faith" but one that he could believe in himself. I reread the entry that had so touched me because of its selflessness. It was a passage that lamented the death of an innocent man. I shivered as I realized, in many ways, how close it would parallel Saffron's own death.

This was his journal entry for March 23, during the season of Lent. In six months he would enter the Citadel.

For years my mother has been dragging me to church. I've heard about Christ on the cross numerous times. And it's never affected me.

Until yesterday. Just out of curiosity I read in the library about how you died when you were crucified. It's a gruesome death. Why don't they talk much about that in church? Instead, all you see is a clean, polished cross up on the wall behind the pulpit. After enough Sundays, it just fades into the background.

Then last night I dreamed I was on a cross. That soldiers had laid me on my back. One kneeled on my chest to keep me from moving while another held my arm in place. Then another soldier took a big hammer and smashed some spikes through my hands. First one arm and then the other was nailed in place. The spikes through my ankles hurt the most because they broke bones as they went through my body.

It was worse on the cross. As soldiers played dice games below me, I felt like I was suffocating. Because I was hanging from my arms and my diaphragm wouldn't work right. Then, just when I was about to suffocate, I'd put my weight on the broken bones of my ankles to give myself enough support to suck in air. And when I couldn't bear that pain any longer, I went back to hanging on my arms until I started to suffocate again.

It was the most horrible nightmare I've ever experienced. I woke up sweating and crying. And I couldn't go back to sleep. I kept thinking about how Jesus actually died on the cross. From exhaustion and dehydration and suffocation.

And in the darkness, I said out loud, "My God, how could I bear this? How did you bear this?"

That's when I first started really thinking about God as mine. Someone personal, who walked the earth in a human's shoes. Someone who cared enough for me and everyone else in the world that he chose to enter into our pain, rather than simply observing it from above.

What haunts me the most is knowing that Jesus had a chance to tell Pilate that he was innocent.

But he didn't. He kept his silence.

Even though he, as God's Son, knew how horrifying it would be for the spikes to go through his hands and *through the bones of his ankles and how he would die in the worst way possible.*

And yet he allowed it to happen.

The wondering haunts me more than how terrible the cross was.

As soon as I opened the door of my rental car on Sally Morrison's property, I smelled cats. Or, more accurately, since they are reputed to be clean animals, I smelled the evidence of cats.

Sally Morrison's double-wide trailer had not been difficult to find. It was at the end of a winding road that cut through mesquite and sand to the top of a hill overlooking the town. Neon glowed from the three casinos below, and stars burned bright, white holes in the black above. Venus hung low, and I had to watch it for a few moments to decide that its brightness was not the approach of a jet's landing lights on its descent to Vegas. The edges of the desert mountains in the distance seemed like folds of dark velvet beneath a half-moon.

Beautiful as the view was, I doubted that visitors enjoyed it, given the ammonia pungency of cat urine that pervaded the area.

Because curtains were drawn, the windows of the double-wide gave meager light, and I stumbled on the uneven ground as I walked toward it. It helped little that I was carrying two small bags of cat food. They'd been expensive because I'd purchased them at a convenience store.

At least I was armed with the proper gifts; three cats scattered as I took the rickety steps up to the trailer door.

Lucille Ball's laughter greeted me. A cat wandered out the pet flap cut into the door. It rubbed up against my leg, then disappeared into the darkness behind me. I set down the cat food and knocked loudly to be heard above the television inside.

Silence greeted the knock, as if the volume of the television had been abruptly turned down.

I knocked again.

The door cracked open, releasing an even more pungent cat smell. A chain kept the door from opening farther.

"I'm looking for Marcella Morrison," I said, slightly out of breath.

"I've got a shotgun. Pointing right at the door. It'll shoot right through if you're here to try anything funny."

My stomach muscles tightened involuntarily. "I've got two bags of cat food and a simple question for you."

"Ain't such a thing as a simple question from a man." Her voice wheezed. Cigarette smoke drifted through the inch-wide crack of the open door. It was a welcome alternative to the other smell. "Trust me; I know."

"I'd like to slide a photo inside," I said. "If you can tell me anything about the woman, I'd sure appreciate it."

"How much money you got? I don't help anyone for nothing. Never have. Never will."

"Depends." I pushed the photo through the door and held it in place, grateful that the door provided a barrier of sorts for this conversation. "How much help can you give?"

The photo was plucked from my fingers.

I waited.

"Come inside," the wheezy voice said moments later. I heard the chain slide open. "A hundred dollars will buy you as much conversation as you need. Shotgun was a bluff," Sally said.

Her dark eyes were lost in the puffiness of her face, and her skin seemed as cracked and fissured as the desert gullies outside. Her lost glories were further emphasized by thick hair dyed black, the hair of a woman half her age. She sat on an old red couch in a tattered robe, bound tightly by her arms crossed in front of her chest. Two fat gray cats jumped onto her lap.

Fifteen, maybe more, other cats occupied different perches in the trailer. The tang of their cat litter was so strong my skin felt greasy.

"What do you want to know about Patricia McNamera?" she said. A cigarette burned in the ashtray set on a table beside the couch. "Nice girl, actually. Talked like you. Good body too. I told her a hundred times to go to Vegas and dance."

"She have her son with her?" I asked.

"Where's my hundred?"

I pulled out my wallet. Set two twenties and a ten on the table beside the ashtray.

She leered. "Half down, half when I deliver, huh?"

"About her son," I said.

"Teenager. Real brat. Drove an old beater like he was in a stock-car race."

I stood and took my money off the table. "Thanks for your time. Cat food's still yours."

"Relax, little boy." She cackled. "Her daughter was maybe

two years old. So you know enough about her to call my bluff. What do you want with her?"

"Just want to find her."

"It's been what, twenty years?" Marcella said. "You're sniffing a cold trail."

"I'm on a trail, though."

"What was she running from? I've always wanted to know."

I set the money back down. "I believe this money is in exchange for answers to *my* questions."

"Not as interested in the money as you might think. My Social Security covers what I need for the cats. My property here is paid for. And I only work at the Star-Spangled so I won't get too crazy from isolation. I liked Patricia. You're not going to find out anything about her if I think you want to hurt her."

"She was running," I said, "from an abusive husband. And from something she knows about the death of a young man."

Marcella Morrison leaned over, took a long drag of her cigarette, and studied me through squinting eyes. Forty years earlier, she might have successfully pulled off the classy-dame act. Now, however, she was an almost hideous caricature of a vixen in a black-and-white detective movie.

I leaned forward, hoping her cigarette smoke would drift my way and cover the cat smell, and waited for her to come to her decision.

"Her little girl, Lizzie, was only a couple of years old when they moved here," Marcella said. "Never talked about where they came from or why. Patricia wasn't interested in anything except waitressing and getting home to her girl. Plenty of men hit on her, but she ignored them. Then one day, maybe two or three years later, a man walks into the Star-Spangled. Tired, like he'd been driving plenty. He's reading a newspaper when she walks up to take his order. He looked at her; she looked at him. Like each had just been shot. He calls her by a different name. Victoria." Marcella's eyes gleamed from the folds of her fleshy cheeks. "Scored right now with that, didn't I?"

I nodded.

"See, that's why I remember her so good. She comes into a one-horse town and doesn't say much about where and why. Then leaves again when some man calls her by a different name. Made all of us curious, but there wasn't anything to do about it after she was gone."

"She left right away?"

"Honey, that afternoon. Told that man up and down he had it wrong. That her name was Patricia. Left the table. Walked through the kitchen, out the back door, packed up all she could from the trailer, drove out of town. Didn't even call for her paycheck, from wherever it was she went." Marcella scratched one cat, then another. "Her neighbor, though, had an interesting story. It should be worth another fifty bucks, if you want it."

For someone who wasn't interested in money, she went to great efforts to disguise the fact.

"Sure," I said. "You give receipts?"

She cackled, then coughed. "No receipts. Just a story."

I pulled out my wallet again.

"The neighbor saw Lizzie on the front steps. Midafternoon, and, honey, when it's hot here, nobody stays outside. Lizzie was maybe four or five by then. Neighbor's thinking maybe Lizzie is locked out and goes up to help. Right by the door, she hears Patricia on the phone. Almost yelling. Word for word, plain, so the neighbor got everything."

Marcella paused significantly. I pulled out a fifty.

"Something about bodies under a lodge. Something about Freemasons and if they come looking, she'll let the world know about where to find them and who put them there. You think maybe that gave us something to gossip about for six months, right on the heels of Patricia driving away with Lizzie and never coming back?"

"I can see why," I said, hoping my voice didn't squeak from the urge to cough. I needed more cigarette smoke to disguise the cat smell. "You never heard from her again?"

"Never. She left the trailer she rented, all her furniture behind. Pots and pans. Everything. Didn't even ask for her rent deposit back, far as I know."

"Did she have any friends here before she left?"

Marcella puffed on her cigarette. With her other hand, she ruffled the fur of a cat in her lap again. "You mean anyone else that's lived here long enough you can ask them questions too?"

"Yes."

"No one I can think of. She kept to herself, mainly. Except for Rachel Metcalf. About her age. Worked at the Star-Spangled too. Had a little girl about Lizzie's age named Jennifer. They spent time together, probably because back then wasn't too many playmates in Searchlight for either of the little girls. And both of them, Patricia and Rachel, were churchgoers. Another reason it was fun to gossip about those buried bodies. Patricia wearing a cross and never working Sundays because she wanted to go to church, but having a dark secret like that."

"Any chance you know where I could find Rachel?"

"If it's true about heaven like her and Patricia believed, you'll have to find a way to get there. A couple of months before Patricia left, Rachel and her husband and daughter died in a house fire. Worst thing that any of us old-timers can remember."

I moved toward the door. Although I'd flown almost across the country for this conversation, I was desperate to flee the interior of this cat hole.

"That's probably worth that first hundred, don't you think?" Marcella coughed again and swallowed with a grimace.

I gave her the remaining fifty.

Anything to buy my freedom.

C H A P T E R

21

Much as I wanted to sleep, I decided to take a red-eye back to Atlanta. My drive from Searchlight to Vegas returned me to the airport in plenty of time to catch the flight. Once I was in the air, I wandered to the back of the airplane and found three seats across that were open. I discreetly removed my prosthesis, lifted the armrests so I could lie across all three seats, and slept lightly until the pilot announced our descent.

In Atlanta, I had a half hour before my connecting flight into Charleston. I clutched a coffee and staggered like a zombie to the gate, highly aware by the reaction of people who passed close by that the musk of pungent cat clung to the clothes I'd slept in.

All told, I arrived in Charleston about eighteen hours after I'd first stepped onto an airplane to leave it. In those

eighteen hours, I'd taken four flights, flown close to five thousand miles, driven another one hundred and fifty miles, and
interviewed two waitresses. The life of the private investigator
was not as glamorous as television led me to believe.

I reached my house just in time to drive Angel to school.

✢

"Nick, I think friends need to be honest with each other,"
Angel said. She rolled down the window to the Jeep before I
could get it out of first gear. "Even with the top down, I need
more air. If you're going to visit Kellie this morning, you might
want to shower first." She paused. "And maybe shave too. That
gray hair on your chin . . ."

"Thanks, Angel. And it's not all gray. Did you get your
homework finished last night?"

She sniffed. "And is that cigarette smoke on you?"

"It is."

"You didn't smoke, did you?"

"No."

"Nick, you do a bad job of lying."

"I wasn't smoking. Someone in the room was," I explained.

She squinted at me in suspicion. "If that's a lie, you put a
lot of work into thinking it through. Just promise me you won't
smoke, all right? It's not good for you."

"Promise. Now tell me about your homework."

I knew the answer already. Angel had been taught by her
grandmother that education was the key to freedom, and she
was nearly fanatic about getting the best grades possible. So

she talked on about what she was learning, and I enjoyed listening to her animated voice. After news about school, she said, "Not only that, but I put in some time on the new Web site for Glennifer and Elaine."

"Oh." This was a surprise to me. "They agreed to your business proposal?"

I turned up Church Street, going past the rainbow-colored houses that had once been the quarters for slaves.

"Not yet," Angel said. "But soon enough they will. You can bet on that."

"Really? How much do you want to put on it?"

"Twenty dollah, no hollah," she said, going into her street-slang accent.

"You got it." I grinned.

We drove in relative silence for a few minutes until we passed the market area, where horses stood patiently in their harnesses to carriages. Early morning tourists were gathered in clusters, waiting for tours of the historic streets.

"Nick?"

"Angel."

"You think maybe we can talk through this school thing? I miss my friends."

Her voice reflected sadness, and I thought I understood. She'd agreed to try a different school, away from the run-down public school she'd attended while living with her grand-mother.

"We can talk about it," I said. "Now? Tonight? You just tell me when, and I'll be an elephant."

"Elephant?"

"All ears," I explained.

She giggled. It was one of the things that I loved about her. That she could be so grown-up one moment and so young the next.

"How about tonight?" she said. "Maybe by then you'll have found time to shower."

✛

The housekeepers were gone; they left a note saying they had taken Maddie with them to go grocery shopping.

I showered. The warm water left me with a sense of tired well-being, and all I wanted was a couple hours of sleep. But I'd promised to visit Kellie as soon as possible. I wasn't optimistic about my accomplishments to report, but Kellie soon proved my pessimism wrong.

"Hey," she said with enthusiasm as I stepped into the hospital room.

I worked up a smile.

"You look tired."

"Am," I said.

The bruises on her face had begun to clear. She was sitting straighter. "Sounded tired, too, on your voice-mail message for me."

"Wanted to leave you the information from Vegas before I got onto the plane for Atlanta."

"Afraid the plane would crash?" she teased.

I didn't have the energy for banter. "Actually, yes. I hate flying. It's unnatural. Except for birds, bats, insects, and some squirrels."

"Well, thanks," she said. "For the information. And for getting it to me. I've been working since I got up this morning. I've got some good news and bad news."

I sat beside the bed. "Mind if I have some water?"

She nodded. I listened as I sipped.

"Patricia and Lizzie McNamera," she said. "New names for Victoria and Sophia Sebastian. I've been able to start trace work on them. With my laptop and the Internet and my cell phone, I've learned in a couple of hours what used to take a couple of weeks."

My mouth still felt dry from exhaustion. I continued to sip.

"The good news is that I found all the records I needed on them and their time in Nevada," she said. "There was a Nevada driver's license under the McNamera name and also a Social Security number registered to Patricia McNamera. Everything was legit, by the way. Down to a birth certificate for Elizabeth, who also had a legitimate Social Security number."

"You're telling me their new identities were that good?"

"They could both have applied successfully for passports."

"So we should be able to find them."

Kellie shook her head. "Here's the bad news. Just after she skipped out of Searchlight, it's like both their names vanished. Never used again, at least not in a way that matched their Social Security numbers. We've got nothing to track down where they moved to."

"Hang on," I said. "Doesn't that mean everything *seemed* legit? She was Victoria Sebastian. So she had to get fake ID if she wanted to be someone else."

Kellie smiled. "*Was* legit. Whoever got them their identification papers—and it's not as hard as you might think to find someone to do that in any major city—did it the hard way. Found the birth records of a mother and daughter that roughly matched their ages. Sent away for duplicate birth certificates, then used those to get new Social Security cards. From that base, it's easy to build up the rest of an identity."

I put my water down. "Sure. Except whoever happens to be the real owners of those birth certificates might get cranky when they find out that someone is living in their shadows. And doesn't the Social Security department start wondering why contributions are coming into the same account from two different sources?"

"Not if the real Patricia and Elizabeth McNamera are already dead."

My thoughts felt like rumbling rocks moving through my skull. "Already dead? As in go out and kill someone so you can steal their identities?"

"Not quite, Nick. But close."

I rubbed my temples. "Spell it out for me. Please."

"Think of the identity thieves as ghouls. They look through death records to find someone dead with roughly the same birth date as the person who needs a new identity. The chances of the government bureaucracy at any level matching birth records with death records are extremely remote. If you start with death records from a different state, you've made it almost impossible for the overlap to be discovered. If you only need one identity, it's relatively easy. But two . . ."

She paused, pulled something up on her laptop screen, and began to read it aloud for me. " 'Nineteen seventy-seven.

Family of four dies in an apartment fire in Cincinnati. Tom McNamera; wife, Patricia; daughter Elizabeth; and a baby girl named Mary.' As I said, once Victoria had the birth certificates for both of them, it was easy to legitimately apply for the rest. Driver's license, Social Security cards . . ."

I nodded. "So Victoria becomes Patricia, living in Nevada."

"My guess is that John Sebastian set her up," she said. "Slick."

"Sure. So slick that all they needed to do was duplicate the trick after abandoning Nevada. Find another mother and daughter of similar ages who died, and go from there. Two new birth certificates, two new identities."

For the first time since walking into the room, I smiled. Perhaps all that flying had been worthwhile. I was about to tell Kellie why when she reached across and took my hand.

"I like that smile, Nick."

Startled, I did my best to remain bland.

"I think you know me well enough to know that I'm used to doing things myself. I don't like to lean on anyone. I don't like that position of vulnerability. But . . ."

With her fingers, she lifted my fingers apart, and played with them, up and down.

"Because the accident put me here, I didn't have any choice but to ask you to help, and you've done it without making me feel like I owe you. Or that you're doing it for any other reason than to genuinely help a friend."

"That's because—"

"Shhh. I've been working up my nerve to do this for the

last day." Her smile, even with her jaw wired shut, was beautiful and alluring. "And even if I don't look afraid, I am."

My mouth was suddenly dry. But with her fingers intertwined with mine, it did not seem like the moment to take another drink of water.

"Anyway," she said, "I want to say thanks. And that I know you well enough to believe you would never try to impose on me for the help you've given. And there's the irony. The more help you give me, the less likely you'd take a step to move us beyond friendship, because you'd be afraid it would be like forcing me to go someplace I don't want to go."

She pulled me forward, gently kissed my forehead, then pushed me away. "There," she said, "just so you know I've taken the first step."

"Um, thanks," I said.

"No, Nick. This is not a moment for your reserved politeness. It is a movie moment. Where you lean forward and kiss my forehead. So that I know you've taken the step with me. So I don't feel like an idiot for making the first move." She was smiling.

I paused. Thought furiously. Kellie was a friend, but to me, just a friend. Evidently she had something else in mind. And I needed to be enough of a friend to be straight with her, even if it hurt.

"There's another man in your life," I said slowly. "You haven't talked much about him. He hasn't come back from California to be with you. But as far as I know, he's still in your life."

I said it very quietly. It was the right thing to say. And the right time. But also the wrong thing to say. At the wrong time.

She blinked a few times. Withdrew her fingers from mine. "You're right, Nick. Stupid me."

"I—"

"You're right. He's sold a screenplay. Found a starlet for a girlfriend. He's out of my life and picked the aftermath of my car accident to phone and finally tell me that he's been with that girl for months already. But you're right. Hearing that from him today is a poor excuse to choose you as a rebound target. We'll just rewind a few minutes and pretend it didn't happen."

Her voice was so neutral, I knew she was angry. Maybe with me. Maybe with herself. But definitely angry.

"I—"

"Nick, shift to Patricia McNamera. Who dropped out of life when she fled from Searchlight, Nevada. You spoke with a friend of hers there. Any hints at all where she might have gone?"

"Rachel and Jennifer Metcalf," I said. The softness of Kellie's fingers had left such an impression on my hand that it felt like they were still caressing mine. "I think I remember their names correctly. They died in a house fire in Searchlight. Rachel was about Victoria's age, and Jennifer was Sophia's age. They died only months before Victoria left town. If she'd learned from the first time how to make a new identity, maybe she decided to use theirs."

"Good. I'll get right on that. Shouldn't be difficult." She spoke quickly, matter-of-factly. "I'll put a call in to the sheriff there, get him to confirm the names. Then start searching my databases."

"Kellie . . ." She didn't have a boyfriend now. Should I try to make it right between us, even if it was a risk?

She gave me a polite smile. "Nick, we're a team right now. Our focus is finding Victoria Sebastian."

"Kellie . . ."

"And don't worry," she said. "If we find out what happened to Matt, you'll get half of the reward that Danielle Pederson offered my firm."

"Kellie . . ."

"Keep your cell phone handy, Nick. I'll call you as soon as I get any results. If I do, will you be able to fly out on short notice?"

"The housekeepers are there to help with Angel and Maddie," I said. "Just like last night."

"Good."

My cell phone rang. I glanced at the caller ID. "It's Jubil."

"Answer it." She waved me away. "See you later."

I began to walk to the door. As difficult as it was, I refused to stop and turn and look and try to talk with her one last time.

"Jubil," I said into the phone as I stepped out of Kellie's room, "how's it going?"

"Good," he answered. "You?"

"Fine," I lied. "Just fine."

C H A P T E R

22

"I looked into the truck driver's background like you told me to yesterday," Jubil said. "The one who hit Kellie."

"Not told. Suggested."

I leaned against my Jeep in the parking lot of the hospital. Jubil stood beside me, arms crossed. He had called my cell from here, then waited for me to walk here from Kellie's hospital room.

The temperature had started to rise, and the clouds had cleared. The drone of a big, lumbering bomber descending to the military base provided background noise to the traffic on the nearby street.

"As you *suggested,*" Jubil said, "I found out as much as I could about the truck driver. Big sports fan. Thinks he knows a lot about it, which in itself isn't bad or unusual. Puts him in good company with half the males over age ten in this country. This one, though, likes to bet according to his sports wisdom. Now he's down to 10 or 20 percent of the males. But he falls into the compulsive-gambling category, and that makes him both stupid and criminal."

"He tell you that?"

"His recent ex-wife. By the time he'd secretly put a second and then a third mortgage on the house, she'd had enough."

I nodded.

"Now get this. Three days after the accident, the house is paid off. In full. Two hundred grand."

"So the accident was a setup. Someone paid him to do it."

"Not so fast, my junior-grade sidekick. We bring this guy down to the station, and he claims he hit it big on a few smart bets. We ask him for the bookies to back up his story, and he tells us it was offshore Internet gambling. Dead end for us. If he sticks to the story, all we have him for is failing to stop for a stop sign, various vehicular misdemeanors and crimes. Insurance covers all damages, so the downside for him, max, he serves six months soft time. More than likely, he gets fined, loses his license. You tell me, is that worth a couple hundred thousand?"

I did the math and snorted. "Six months in jail. Like getting paid more than fifteen thousand a month to sit around and watch television while someone delivers your meals."

Jubil uncrossed his arms and walked the few short steps to his unmarked Chevy, parked behind my Jeep. "If Kellie had died in the accident, then he's looking at involuntary manslaughter," he said over his shoulder. "Courts are backed up so bad he could plea-bargain it to maybe three years, serve a year, and get parole."

"Which means he gets paid two hundred grand a year to sit in jail."

"Yup." Jubil had reached through his open window into the passenger side of his car. He returned to me with a stack of papers. "Look through this," he said.

I flipped a couple of pages, saw too much typeface on the papers. "How about the *Reader's Digest* version?" The two-hour nap on the plane had barely staved off my sense of sleep deprivation. My clumsiness with Kellie in the hospital hadn't helped. I didn't have much energy for concentration.

"Reports of similar accidents in Charleston and this area over the last forty years. I mean, *very* similar. Car at stop sign. Big truck runs into the back end, spins it into busy traffic. Driver of car dead or seriously injured. Including the accident that killed Ethan Osgoode."

"Let me guess. Accidents spaced out in a way that the similarities aren't obvious unless someone really looks for them."

"Yup. Any idea how many traffic fatalities we have each year in a fifty-mile radius of Charleston? Now think about all the different jurisdictions and departments in charge. Chances of the accidents being linked are so remote as to be not worth considering."

"A semi," I said. "The perfect murder weapon. Driver of it won't get hurt. Unlike other murders, the driver doesn't even try to get away or hide the fact he did it. Simply takes whatever punishment the law delivers and walks away with the money."

"Remember, we're just speculating," Jubil said. He tapped

the stack of papers. "Of course, this has some backgrounds on some of the truck drivers involved. Sixty percent of those drivers had previous criminal records. Some served time for manslaughter; some didn't. The other 40 percent? Haven't had time to look into their backgrounds. What are the odds, you think, of some of them like the one who hit Kellie? Secret vices that make them desperate enough to accept payment for running into the back end of someone's car at a stop sign."

"If this is true," I said, "that means Kellie was a threat to someone. She'd found out something that could hurt or expose them. Right?"

"You got it, pal. Which means, chances are, you're now a threat too."

C H A P T E R

23

My early morning flight into Chicago's O'Hare Airport was just the opposite of what I'd expected. The weather was balmy, almost springlike. The flight was smooth and on time. My taxi driver—college-aged and shaved bald—didn't inflict his solutions for world peace on me. Traffic from O'Hare to the downtown Loop was free of jams.

The driver stopped at the corner of Madison and LaSalle. "Take all day," he said with a grin. "I love getting paid not to drive."

"I may be back right away. Depends on if I'm going to meet the right person."

I opened the door.

"Old flame?" he asked.

"Little more complicated than that."

He snorted. "Nothing's more complicated than old flames."

I stepped out of the car.

The address was a high-rise apartment in a posh neighborhood. I walked up the steps to the lobby.

A middle-aged doorman greeted me. "Whom will you be visiting this morning?"

I told him.

"Is she expecting you?"

I told him no.

I handed the doorman a folded twenty. "When you call to tell her she has a visitor," I said, "please tell her my name is Nick Barrett. And that I'm here on behalf of Victoria Sebastian and Patricia McNamera."

"Certainly."

His bow was as discreet as the way he palmed the twenty.

Michigan Avenue snaked far below, with cars like toys as they leapfrogged from lane to lane, from the shadow of one high-rise to another. The lake itself stretched to the horizon, a deep blue beneath a cloudless sky.

I studied all of it until the noise of shoes on hardwood told me that my hostess had returned.

"Nice view," I said. I assumed that such a comment was expected of all visitors to this luxury apartment.

"No small talk. Please. Don't pretend your presence here is something that it's not."

I turned to Rachel Van Doren, who was holding a tray

with china cups on saucers, a silver coffeepot, a creamer, and a sugar bowl. She had once lived in Charleston in front of a much, much smaller lake.

Although she had aged a quarter century since the last photograph I'd seen of her and her hair was much shorter now, she was unmistakably Victoria Sebastian. The blonde hair was now fashionable platinum, the cheekbones still elegant and striking. She wore an expensive sweat suit—I'd caught her about to go to the workout center in the building—and either spent a considerable amount of money on a plastic surgeon or worked out on a very regular basis.

She set the tray on a table between two chairs, sat on one chair, and gestured at the other for me.

"Were there a chopping block between us instead of this table," she said, "I would extend my neck with as much dignity as possible. As it is, I shall only offer you coffee."

There was no smile as she said it.

I accepted the coffee.

She noted my glance around the living room. At the carvings and the paintings.

"My husband is a professor in African studies. He is a good man. And doesn't deserve what I presume will happen to our family in the next weeks."

"And what would that be?" I asked.

"If you've found me, you know better than I what will happen now."

"My guess," I said, choosing my words with care, "is what happens next depends on how much involvement you had with the death of a Citadel cadet named Matthew Pederson."

She tilted her head and stared at me. "Who did you say you were?"

"Nicholas Barrett."

"Not your name. Your work identity. What department? What's your official title? I was so devastated when I heard my doorman announce those names, I forgot to ask for your badge. I simply assumed by the way you were dressed that you were an undercover detective of some sort."

I was in khakis and a black mock turtleneck. The black leather jacket I'd worn was draped over another chair.

"No department," I answered. "No title."

She slumped slightly. "Then I don't understand. Why exactly are you here?"

"I was hired to find the truth behind your disappearance."

"Then it wasn't John. He sent me on my way. Happily. So who hired you?"

I shook my head. "Can't answer that."

"Then you must be here to kill me. If I promise to make it easy for you, will you promise to leave my husband and daughter out of this?"

Her courage in the face of her fear was impressive. It made me wonder if what Sally Morrison had said was true— that the woman she'd known as Patricia McNamera had become a follower of Christ and his message.

"Mrs. Van Doren, I'm not here to harm you. Why don't we talk, and then both of us can decide what will happen next."

She nibbled at the fingernail of her right index finger. Despite her totally put-together appearance, the ends of all her

polished nails were chipped. "You mean you might not go
to the police?"

"I can't make that promise. By all appearances, Matthew
Pederson was murdered. You were one of the last people to be
seen with him. There is no statute of limitations on murder,
and my silence at this point would make me an accessory—
if that's why you fled Charleston."

"If you're not here officially and you won't tell me who
asked you to look for me, and if I'll be speaking to the police
eventually anyhow, why should I tell you anything?"

I answered by pulling a piece of paper out of my pocket
and unfolding it, the paper that Carmen had given to Kellie.
I handed it to her.

Her hands began to tremble as her eyes fell on the photocopy of the medieval cross.

"Is this," I asked, "why you thought I was here to kill you?"

It took her a full minute to speak. "They didn't send you?"
she asked.

"No."

She blinked once, and it was like opening the gates to a
dam. Tears began to roll down her cheeks, and she did nothing
to wipe them away.

I said nothing.

She cried in silence.

I was wired. Not in the sense that my conversation with the
former Victoria Sebastian was being transmitted to anybody

in a van parked on the street. But a microphone was taped to the center of my chest, with a wire that ran under my armpit to a recorder strapped to the small of my back.

Kellie's suggestion.

She had called late the afternoon before, telling me that if her sources were correct, a woman named Rachel Metcalf had lived in Chicago for the past fifteen years, half that time as Rachel Van Doren, wife to Cornelius Van Doren. They had a daughter named Jennifer, the same age Sophia Sebastian would have been.

Since Kellie couldn't be sure it was Victoria, she requested that I make this trip as a preliminary search, telling me that it was more likely I would get information if I showed up without the police.

We debated whether Victoria Sebastian, if indeed she was now Rachel Van Doren, might simply vanish again as soon as I departed. Kellie thought it was less probable now, since she was married and so much time had passed since her disappearance from Charleston.

Given that I had the symbol of the medieval cross, we decided chances were good she would talk, which was why I wore the recording device.

We had also decided that if I learned anything that seemed like it demanded police attention, I would immediately call in the Chicago officials to prevent any flight risk.

In short, we were taking a risk, but one we believed was minimal.

And a risk we hoped would be worthwhile.

I expected Rachel to ask how I'd found her.

She didn't.

"I'm tired of wondering when my past will catch up with me," she said. "And I want my family protected. What can you do to help me?"

I was impressed at how quickly she turned this around and put the pressure on me.

Again, I had to think carefully before answering. I decided I had no answer. Not yet. But I had a question. "What do you think I can do that will help you?"

She answered without hesitation, as if that's exactly where she'd hoped to take me. "Expose them. Without letting them know you've found me."

"Are either of your suggestions possible?"

She nodded. "I believe both of them are." She smiled. Her first since welcoming me into the apartment suites. "As you can imagine, I've been thinking about this for quite some time."

"Why, then," I said, "haven't you acted upon it before?"

Another smile. If she was trying to charm me, it was working. "I thought I could just let sleeping dogs lie."

That made sense to me. Why take the risk until it was necessary? And I'd just made it necessary for her.

"Lately, though, I've been realizing that I need to do something, the right thing. Something happened to me when I lived in Searchlight. I met Rachel, and I met God. Then Rachel died, and I was on the run again. Our friendship and the faith we shared has stayed with me, but so has the fear—of them, of what they could do to my family. I know that nothing I can do now will make what happened to Matthew right. But I have to try."

"Well, then," I said, "tell me how I can help you."

C H A P T E R

24

Traffic back to O'Hare from the Loop was light, and I made it
to the airport in plenty of time to check in for my 1:25 P.M.
flight back to Charleston. But mechanical problems delayed
takeoff. Along with one hundred and fifty other passengers, I
suffered the claustrophobia of sitting in the jet on the runway
for an hour while the plane was fixed, and another half hour
while the paperwork was processed.

I didn't grumble, however. Because of my dislike of
flying, I wanted the pilots to be as prudent as possible. If it
took them half a day to be satisfied that once the jet was in the
air they would be able to land it safely again, I was fine with it.

I did more than grumble, however, upon arrival in
Charleston. The scheduled 4:40 arrival had become nearly
6:30. I stepped out of the airport into the darkness of an early

fall evening. My leg was bothering me because of the long day, and when I reached my Jeep after a walk that felt far too long, I discovered it had been vandalized.

All four tires had been flattened.

I was alone in this corner of the parking lot, and my first reaction was moderate fear. Had this been done to trap me here?

I looked around, expecting footsteps.

None arrived. The scream of a descending jet grew louder. It seemed to pass directly overhead, briefly blotting out the starlight.

I looked back at the tires, hoping I'd seen wrong. But they were still flat. If I hadn't been wearing a prosthetic lower leg, I would have kicked them in frustration. I saw no choice but to walk all the way back to the terminal, glad that at least all I carried was a briefcase.

As I walked, I considered my choices. I decided I was too tired to go through the hassle of calling for a tow truck and waiting. Especially since I'd promised Angel I would get back home as quickly as possible.

As I reached the terminal, a taxi slowed for me. "Need a ride?" the driver called.

I should have been suspicious. For all the driver knew, I was simply going to the terminal to catch a flight. But it was another couple hundred yards to the taxi stand, and my leg was really aching. I was glad to save myself the effort.

"Thanks."

He pulled the taxi closer. I saw an old, wizened man behind the steering wheel. I climbed in the backseat on the left-hand side and gave him my address.

"Sure," he said. He drove in silence past the other taxis, then pulled into the terminal.

Before I could ask why, the other back door opened. Miles Ashby slung his large body inside beside me and slammed the door. The taxi slowly pulled away.

"Good to see you, Nick," Miles said. "Ready for a nice long ride?"

CHAPTER

25

The taxi now picked up speed on the airport exit road. The fluorescent streetlamps cast alternating shades of shadow and orange across Ashby's face as he leaned back against the door, knees tucked in front of him. Even so, his leer was as plain as the pistol that he'd removed from the shoulder holster beneath his suit jacket.

"Payback," he said.

I didn't respond. Obviously it disappointed him.

"Back in the hospital. You sent me into the room to apologize to those kids of yours. And I said I'd make you pay."

"So you did."

I was waiting for the taxi driver to glance into his rearview mirror and notice the pistol that Ashby made no effort to hide.

"Look on the seat between us," Ashby said. "And slowly,

very slowly, pick up one of the tie-down straps. I've got this trigger set at a very light pull weight and would love to use it."

The next wave of orange fluorescent light passed through the interior, and I saw the straps he meant. They were the nylon plastic loops that tightened like a ratchet. Available at any hardware store. That's when I had my first inkling of how real my danger was.

God, please help me, I prayed silently. *Help me be calm, figure out what to do, how to get out of this.* If the straps had already been in the cab waiting for me, I knew this was no random abduction.

I took one of the straps just as we left the airport. Soon the streetlights stopped illuminating the interior.

"Jones," Ashby said in a conversational voice, "it's dark back here. Need some help."

The cabdriver switched on the overhead light. Again I saw Ashby's leer far too clearly. Knew I wouldn't be getting any help from the cabdriver.

"Face away from me," Ashby said. "Hands behind your back. With your right hand, hold the loop. Place your left hand through the loop."

I saw no choice but to obey, even knowing that once my hands were secured behind my back, I would be totally helpless.

When I turned around, my head was nearly up against the window. The taxi was moving at about thirty miles an hour. I felt my knee against the door handle. I tested it by pushing upward. It gave. I decided if we slowed at all, I would pop the handle and dive through the open door, taking my chances on hitting the pavement. At this moment, however, I remained compliant. I held the loop with my right hand and slid my left hand through it.

Ashby slid forward. I felt the pistol barrel grind into my lower back.

"Tempted to blow out a kidney," Ashby said. "Give me an excuse, will you? Be therapeutic for me."

I did not give him an excuse. I took what little comfort I could in the sensation of the door handle above my knee.

"Right hand through the loop now," Ashby said.

I did as told.

"Good boy," he said. "Hold steady."

He pulled the end of the strap, and with the little snap-snap-snap sound, he tightened it. I pushed my hands together to keep my wrists slightly apart, trying to keep some slack. It fooled him, probably because the interior light above put the area in front of him in darkness. I'd managed to keep my wrists about an inch apart. My hands wouldn't be able to slide through the gap, but at least I would keep blood circulating. I hoped I would live long enough to make that relevant.

The taxi began to slow for a stoplight.

"He's wrapped good," Ashby said. "Don't need the light now."

I knew there was traffic behind me. If there was a time to escape, this was it. As the driver hit the light switch, as the new darkness temporarily distracted Ashby.

I jammed my knee upward and popped my shoulder into the door.

Nothing happened, except for Ashby's laughter.

"Automatic door lock," he said. "Now turn around and slowly swing your feet toward me."

Again I was a compliant prisoner. Hands behind my back, shoulders leaning against the window, I lifted my legs in his direction.

He took the second strap, looped it around my ankles, and pulled it tight. This time, I pressed my heel against the bottom of my prosthesis. It earned me a half inch of slack.

"Feet back on the floor," he said. "Look straight ahead."

I did. The taxi was gaining speed again, heading toward the I-26 southbound exit.

"This is where it gets fun," Ashby said. He holstered his pistol and took a switchblade out of the inner pocket of his suit coat. Flicking open the blade, he held it below window level.

"My first choice would be this," he said. "But Jones says he has a better way. Still, I might just make you bleed a little. Ever see the movie *Chinatown*, where the guy gets his nostril cut?"

"Not in the car." I was surprised at the clearness of the command that Jones gave. And that it came from behind me, from the stereo speakers mounted beneath the back window. "Do you have any idea how easy it is for even a bad forensic team to find blood?"

I did not like the implication that there might be a need for a forensic team. Suddenly, it mattered a lot less to me that I'd discovered so many answers behind the disappearances of Matthew Pederson and Victoria Sebastian.

All of a sudden I was thinking about death. *My* death.

It's strange, when you're facing death, how many bits and pieces of conversations and interactions go through your head. As I sat as a prisoner in that speeding taxi, my thoughts were still focused on solving the mystery of Anson Saffron's death and Matthew Pederson's disappearance.

All stories, as you know, involve the interaction of human needs and wants—for the two are surely inseparable—and the interaction of all human needs and wants becomes stories. The interaction—from the criminal and deplorable to the heroic and laudable—usually becomes an intricate, complicated web. And each person has his or her own perspective and knowledge of the events. To get to the center of the web is a simple matter of hearing the stories from all the involved parties.

While this is simple, it's not necessarily easy. And the darker the story, the more difficult this task becomes. The key to unlocking each person's secret is motivation. Sometimes direct evidence makes denial useless. Sometimes it is the leverage of understanding other pieces of the story.

With Victoria Sebastian, it was the fact that she'd been found after all these years.

It had taken her over an hour to explain her role in Matthew Pederson's disappearance. She'd told me about the first evening she, under the direction of the society, had introduced herself to Matthew Pederson, senior cadet at the Citadel.

She'd gone to the bar, one of the Citadel students' hangouts, and found that the information given her was indeed accurate. Matthew was there, sitting in a corner and watching the pool games. When he finally made a trip to the washroom in the rear of the bar, she'd placed herself in his path.

She discovered that, unlike his friends, he was drinking not alcohol but Coke. That, unlike his friends, when he returned to the corner, he didn't assess her stunning beauty and make suggestive comments. That, unlike his friends, he wanted to be alone in the noise and the crowd.

It took her much more effort than she expected to begin a relationship. She found this humorous in a way. Here she was, a woman who had just five years earlier competed in the Miss South Carolina contest, and she'd found it difficult to win a college student's attention and then time with him for conversation.

While his friends leered from the safety of their pack, she spent time in another corner of the bar with Matt and discovered too that Matthew Pederson was not the swaggering big man on campus she'd been led to expect.

Although she had her assignment, she found herself drawn to him. What she wanted to conquer, of course, were his secrets.

That was a Friday night. On Saturday night, she reappeared at the same bar. As did he. This time he walked directly toward her, a bee drawn by fragrant blossoms.

They huddled together, sharing intimate conversation, the noise of the bar giving them total privacy. Neither drank alcohol. Simply ordered Cokes to keep the waitress happy and let those drinks fizz into flatness.

It was on the following weekend that he began to share his misery about a freshman cadet named Anson Hanoway Saffron.

We were on the interstate now, and again streetlights showed Ashby's face. I saw legitimate disappointment. And understood in that moment how badly he wanted to hurt me.

Ashby folded the blade back into the knife's handle and tucked it in his jacket pocket.

"Check his briefcase," Jones said. "Make sure he's got the diary he told the broad in the hospital about."

I flinched.

"That's right," Ashby said. "We know about the diary. I've recorded every word you've said to Mixson. On the phone. In her room. Everything. Even that tender moment when you so nobly told her that she was in a relationship and you couldn't kiss her. Ha."

I tried to recall what I'd told her from Chicago before boarding the airplane. I hadn't been able to reach her until fifteen minutes before the flight, so it had been a brief conversation. *Yes,* I'd said. *Van Doren is Victoria Sebastian. I know why she left Charleston and who's behind it. But there's more. Way more. It's in the diary that belonged to Anson Hanoway Saffron. It will be easier for me to explain once you've read it. They've just called for final boarding. . . .*

Ashby reached for the briefcase at my feet. I thought of trying to head butt him. But he pushed my right shoulder with his left hand to keep me steady and away from him.

There wasn't much in the briefcase. My cell phone, wallet. And the leather-bound diary. I'd read it twice on the flight.

Ashby dumped the contents on the seat between us and dropped the briefcase at his feet. He scooped up the wallet first.

"Hope you have plenty of cash," he said, slipping it into his suit jacket. "You're not going to need it, and I don't mind making sure it doesn't go to waste."

Jones turned on the cab light again. "The diary."

Ashby flipped through it. "It's here."

Jones put us back in darkness again.

"Hey," Ashby said, "we've got a little time. Why don't I tell you how stupid you are. And all about me and Jones."

"Shut up," Jones said from the other side of the Plexiglas.

"Is it really going to make a difference?" Ashby asked him.

The silence from Jones was the answer I didn't want to hear. Because it told me exactly what they intended to do with me.

As the taxi moved down the interstate toward Charleston, Miles bragged about the events of his last few days, and I learned about how and why he and Jones were together.

I didn't give it my full attention.

I knew I was going to die. But not how.

And I feared the worst.

It wasn't the actual dying that bothered me. For over the past months, I had come to grips with what Anson Hanoway Saffron had known: Everyone dies, and I too would die. I had also, after significant struggle, made my peace with God and my past. I was now walking with him. I knew that when I died, whether caused by car crash, plane crash, or simple old age, I would go to heaven.

248

But somehow, I hadn't thought it would be this soon. Or that I'd feel so unprepared for the moment of my death.

C H A P T E R

26

As I sat trussed up in that taxi, my thoughts strayed to Anson Hanoway Saffron and to the journal entry that I'd read on the plane. It was from May 22, and Anson Hanoway would enter the Citadel in September of that year. This was his recording of his life's transformation.

> *It is so difficult to describe. I feel like a snake sliding out of*
> *old skin, like suddenly I have gone from seeing the world*
> *in black and white to vision where wonderful colors exist.*
> *Like I was able to dive into a clean, cool pool of water*
> *from the edge of a desert that took me years to cross.*
>
> *Today I let go.*
>
> *Prayed. Asked God to forgive my sins through his Son,*

Jesus. The one who died such a terrible death on the cross for me. I promised to try to follow him and his example.

Now, suddenly, I can breathe deep, great breaths. And I know that this is what I was born for. It's my destiny, my soul's destiny, to find God. There's this peace because I know that God's in control. And hope, because I know that when I die, it's not the end. And purpose, too, because no matter what kind of job or life I have, my life's foundation is to share the joy of this love.

And I'm free.

Free at last of worrying about what it means to be the son of my father and having to do everything the Saffron way.

Is this part of it too? That I feel so strong inside? That I can stand up to anything on this earth?

That's what life came down to for Anson. Peace, hope, purpose. Believing wasn't just some talisman to get him into heaven at the end of his earthly life. It was a foundation for life on this earth. He saw the life beyond, in one way, as just a continuation, and in another way, as a homecoming.

Peace. Hope. Purpose. In dying to himself, Anson Hanoway Saffron found out how to live in Christ. Living is about learning to die. Some people take a lifetime to understand this. Some never learn it at all. And some, like Anson Hanoway Saffron, learn it early.

Now I was about to find out if what I believed could sustain me too. Did I truly believe that God was the God of the entire universe? And that he was the one, not me, with an eternal perspective? Would I trust him even in this dark situation? Through what remained of my life? And through the looming certainty of death?

Sandwiched between the Citadel and downtown Charleston is a large building that houses the police station, the municipal court, and the South Carolina Department of Transportation. It faces Brittlebank Park and the Ashley River beyond the park. During the day, especially in the summer, families picnic in the shade and enjoy the sweet scent of pine trees. At night, brave teenage couples park in the family sedans of their parents, always conscious of the police building across the street behind them.

It was here that I was taken in the taxi. Jones exited the interstate at Rutledge Avenue and drove past Hampton Park, through the neighborhood where I'd ridden my bicycle as a child to escape the family mansion. Our path next took us past the grounds of the Citadel, where Anson Hanoway Saffron had been found hanging on a cross with a broken chair beneath him.

My sense of helplessness was exacerbated by the fact that the route took me literally within throwing distance of the police station. For all I knew, Jubil was sitting back from his desk at the end of a long day's shift, drinking coffee and exchanging bad jokes with the other detectives. And here I was, about to have my throat cut—or something far worse— by two very bad men.

The taxi's headlights swung across the park's pine trees as Jones turned down the paved road that led to picnic tables and grassy spaces among the trees. We continued, past several parked cars, toward the northern edge of the park, then down a service road that led to the rear of the Charleston RiverDogs' baseball stadium.

My eyes registered a chain-link fence in the headlights, maybe thirty steps back from the service road. Then the engine and headlights shut down. I knew that beyond the fence a large marsh stood on the southwest edge of the Citadel property. A few lights on the far side of the marsh showed the houses of the Citadel's higher-ranking officers.

It was obvious the taxi would go no farther. And very probable that I wouldn't be going much farther, both literally and figuratively. I made a decision to start screaming loudly as soon as they moved me out of the backseat of the cab. With God on my side, I prayed that someone in the parked cars a couple hundred yards away would hear me.

I should have guessed how completely my captors were prepared.

Ashby lifted a roll of duct tape from the floor at his feet. He ripped off a piece and plastered it across my mouth, then patted it gently.

"I really do want to cut you up," he said, almost crooning. "But Jones has a much nastier way to kill you. You'll be an example for everyone else."

I tried to let my anger overwhelm my fear. I did not want to give Ashby any satisfaction.

He patted the duct tape again. "What's the matter, cat got your tongue?"

"Quit playing with your food," Jones said, irritated. "Let's go."

The automatic locks clicked. Ashby opened his door and came around to mine. He pulled me out roughly.

I couldn't walk, of course, so Ashby threw me over his shoulder and carried me in a fireman's lift. He followed the older and much smaller man, who used a flashlight to guide us down a path along a small drainage ditch toward the chain-link fence. The ditch dropped off into a tidal creek that ran parallel with the fence. The fence didn't quite make it to the ditch, so there was room for Ashby to walk around it and then take the remaining few steps to the bank of the tidal creek.

Strange, the details a mind notices, especially when under duress. It was very apparent that they were taking me to a killing place. Yet in the flashlight's spillover, my head bobbing almost against Ashby's stomach, I saw along the bank of the tidal creek a ribbon of curled magnetic tape from a broken cassette, a crushed Budweiser beer can, and barnacles on a log that would be submerged again when the tide rose.

It was only about twenty yards down the tidal creek to a huge square concrete culvert covered with enough soil that grass and shrubs and trees grew above it. Water flowed inland through it, rising about halfway up the pipe. It was tidal water from the Ashley River a hundred yards away, flowing toward the marsh behind the baseball stadium. Later, when the tide shifted, the current would flow out again, toward the river, toward the Atlantic.

Jones stopped and flicked his flashlight beam at the edge of a large cinder block. A short chain was attached to a ring in the block. Fresh chain, glinting in the light. A dog chain with a clip on the end. As if it were ready to be attached to a collar.

"You'll be able to handle this?" he asked Ashby.

"You trying to insult me?"

"By the way you're huffing after carrying him here . . ."

"People who insult me get hurt, old man."

"Just get him ready, the way we planned it."

Ashby dropped his shoulder and let me fall to the ground from waist high. With my hands behind my back, I couldn't protect myself from the fall. I narrowly missed the block and jarred my ribs against a root protruding from the ground. All I was able to do was snort the pain out my nostrils.

Ashby dragged my upper body away from the block. He clipped the end of the chain to the plastic loop around my ankles.

It was then that I realized exactly how I would die. I renewed my pleadings to God. The block of concrete had become an anchor.

"Hey," Ashby said, "give me some light down here. I need a closer look."

Jones obliged.

With my face turned against the grass, I couldn't see what Ashby meant. But I felt a tug on my right shoe.

"His ankle feels weird," Ashby continued.

"Prosthetic," Jones said in a bored voice. "Car accident when he was nineteen. Don't you do any background?"

"You want to throw him in like this?"

"Pull off the fake leg and cinch the loop tighter around his good ankle. One leg will hold him in place just as good as two."

Ashby was smart enough to sit on my good leg as he worked the prosthesis loose. I had no chance to kick him. He finished, threw the prosthesis aside, and pulled the plastic loop tightly around my left ankle. Then he clipped the end of the dog chain to that loop.

"Done," Ashby said. The location of his voice told me that he was still crouched over my feet. "We ready?"

Then without warning, he exhaled violently. His body shuddered and collapsed across my legs.

I twisted to see what had happened.

Jones stood over him, reaching for the long butcher knife in Ashby's upper back.

"Not often I get to do that, let alone with an audience," Jones said. His face was lost behind the light of his flashlight. "Sideways through the ribs. No resistance that way. Takes some skill to find the heart like that, but my old man was a good teacher. Showed me how to hide a knife this big. Showed me how to use it."

He set the flashlight on the ground. I averted my eyes when he tugged at the knife. I heard it splash in the marsh a second or two later.

Jones then rolled Ashby off my legs. He grunted with the effort. Once he had some room, Jones stepped behind Ashby's body and pushed him to the culvert's top edge, then over and into the water. Another splash. Much heavier than the knife's.

"He was such a moron," Jones said. "Such an utter moron."

He turned to me, scanning my face with the flashlight. I blinked against the brightness.

"Won't be that quick for you," he said. "The worse you die, the stronger the message. And the more it will look like they killed you."

From his herringbone jacket he pulled out a medieval-style cross and jammed it into my front pants pocket. "Just so there's no doubt they did it," he said. More to himself than to me.

Without saying more, Jones began to drag the cinder-block anchor toward the lip of the culvert. On my side, hands behind my back, I could do nothing to try to stop him except scrape my fingernails in the dirt. He kept grunting with the effort, wiggling the block side to side to keep it from getting stuck.

With no ceremony, he let it drop over the edge. My half leg flailed uselessly, and the shin of my other leg banged and scraped against the culvert as the weight slowly pulled me down.

Jones moved around to my shoulders. He remained wordless and focused, as if I were already a dead body. Then he lifted my shoulders, so that the upper half of my body was in the air.

And just like that, I fell.

CHAPTER

27

The drop to the water was short, the impact a shock of cold. The heavy cinder block took my legs down quickly, and I futilely sucked air. What difference would it make to survive another thirty or forty seconds before my lungs heaved for oxygen and inhaled dirty, brown river water instead?

With my hands behind my back, I couldn't even flail, useless as the effort would have been with the weight of the block. It settled into the soft mud bottom of the tidal creek. To my amazement, water had not covered me. Instead, it was only above my shoulders, flowing past me with a current that swayed my upper body.

The beam of the flashlight darted along the ground as Jones moved from the top of the culvert to the bank directly beside me. He flashed the light at my head. Then forward to the vertical wall of the culvert, only a couple of feet from me. The light stayed on the wall for long moments, then back to my face, and once more to the wall as if to satisfy himself. I realized he was calculating. And then the reason for his calculations dawned on me.

The water level was now three feet short of the top of the culvert. Only six inches from the top, however, a line of slimy darkness showed how high the tide rose each day. And that line of demarcation was easily above my head. Something Jones was confirming.

At high tide, I would be totally submerged. *Dear God,* I prayed, *do I have to die this way?*

"The horror of it," Jones said then. "After you're found, this city will talk about it for years."

He walked away, using the flashlight beam to pick his way carefully along the bank of the tidal creek. The duct tape was still solidly over my mouth. I couldn't even shout to beg for mercy. Slowly, the flashlight beam grew smaller and smaller as it flitted from side to side. Then it was gone. Like a firefly.

I heard him start the engine. Heard the tires crunch on gravel. Then nothing.

I was alone.

Was this how it had felt for Matthew Pederson at the end of the night he had retired to study, then escaped the Citadel to meet Victoria Sebastian in a taxi? I wondered.

She'd left a message for him, begging to have a few quiet

hours with him along the waterfront. Matthew had wanted
time with her, badly, but felt guilt at his unworthiness. That
night, Matthew had decided idealistically that he must confess
to her his horrible actions. Then it would be her choice. She
could continue seeing him, knowing what he'd done, or flee
him like the monster he believed himself to be.

In the backseat of the taxi, he told her the rest.

How he'd found a diary the night that the four cadets
staged a mock crucifixion. How he'd read it during the day that
followed. How he'd discovered the truth about Ethan
Osgoode, as unaware that this would seal Osgoode's death
sentence as he was that his own had already been determined.

How he'd confronted Osgoode. How Osgoode had
reacted not with shame, but with a leering grin. How Osgoode
had told him about the screws removed from the chair legs,
and how Matthew would be an accessory to murder if Matthew
told anyone else. How Osgoode had reminded him of the
honor of the pact of secrecy among the four senior cadets, and
that by telling anyone else about this, he would violate the pact
and ensure that the other two cadets also would be accessories
to murder. How bringing any of this to light would destroy all
of them.

Matthew told her about his anguish, his conflict of one
honor against another.

He told her how Anson Hanoway Saffron's faith had
touched him. Deeply. How he'd recently chosen the same faith.
And asked forgiveness of the God whom Anson had followed.

Then Matthew had slipped the diary into Victoria
Sebastian's purse, asking her to read it before judging him fully.

After that, the taxi had stopped. Matthew had been so intent on his confession that he had not noticed it had moved to the houses along Colonial Lake. Victoria kissed his cheek lightly—their first physical contact—and asked him to wait in the cab as she retrieved something from the house.

He'd waited inside. Obediently.

And when she stepped out of the cab, the driver had accelerated with Matthew left staring out the back window, calling for her.

Alone.

Except for the driver of the taxi.

Their destination would lead to Matthew's death.

Wind now flagged through dry palmetto leaves, picking up pace, bringing me the sounds of traffic from the bridge over the Ashley a half mile downstream. The water's flow kept pushing me forward, so that, despite the solidness of my anchor, it was difficult to keep my balance on only one foot.

Of all the things to think about while dying, I never expected to be engaged in mental arithmetic. Six-foot tide. Rising and dropping that amount every twenty-five hours? Every twenty-three hours? I knew the cycle changed an hour a day but had forgotten the direction. Forward or back. Decided that the math would be easier if I used, for argument's sake, twenty-four hours. Decided I was a lunatic for focusing on something so trivial when already the water was edging toward the bottom of my chin.

But did I want to think about what would happen as it gradually rose to my nostrils?

Six feet up and down every twenty-four hours, I told myself firmly. If that meant a rise of six feet in twelve hours, then that was half a foot an hour. Six inches every hour. And if I could stretch my neck and keep my head as high as possible, two or three inches until the water first began to trickle into my nostrils?

A half hour left to live. A half hour left to die a thousand times. A half hour left to think of all the things I still wanted to do, to wish for what now could not be on this earth. To think about the growing-closer reality of heaven.

A mental picture drifted into my thoughts. Of my body swaying under the water, my hair lifting and falling with the current. Of my body, when the tide retreated again, slowly settling horizontally in the brackish water before perhaps rising again with the next tide. Falling and rising each day until my body was discovered. It was a grim thought. Long enough undiscovered and the fish would make me unrecognizable. But the Charleston police would have no trouble identifying the cross left in my pants pocket.

Jones was right. It was a death that would become legendary. Spoken of in whispers, even among the jaded aristocracy that pretended no fear of anything.

Had I made the right decision to continue the investigation? Would my discoveries come to light and make any difference in the lives of Rachel, Isabelle, Kellie, or the mysterious person who'd hired us to find Victoria Sebastian? It looked now like I wouldn't live to know. But was this really it? I wondered. Would God help me go peacefully? Or would he send rescue?

Just then a slight sound broke through my thoughts. My eyes had begun to adjust to the darkness, and I saw movement along the bank.

A raccoon. Not much of a rescue party. It stared at me for a few minutes, then moved on.

Strangely, I felt even more lonely.

I could twist around the chain attached to the block and look in different directions. Downstream—inland—the marsh opened up, the swamp grass ghostly white in the moonlight, like a field of wheat dancing with the wind. Beyond it were the lights of the Citadel.

Anson Hanoway Saffron had died there twenty-five years earlier, and because of that, I would die here now.

The water reached my chin, a slowly rising coldness like the grip of death itself. In frustration I lifted and slammed my hands against my back.

Then had a thought.

I slid my hands as far down my back as I could. Had they been more tightly bound, I would not have been able to move them around and below my legs. As it was, I barely made it. I bent over, forcing my face into the water. I lifted my half leg and jammed my wrists below the stump and in front. It allowed me to get my hands partially free. My right arm in front of my body, my left hand behind. Still attached to each other by the loop of plastic. But I was stooped so badly that my face was submerged.

I quickly dropped my hands and wiggled my wrists so that

both hands were behind my body again. I straightened and gasped for breath. Water streamed off my face from my hair.

Now the level was above the bottom of my chin.

I tried to visualize the metal clip attached to the plastic loop around my ankle. Could I reach it with my right hand? I took a deep breath and exhaled. Again and again, trying to force as much oxygen into my blood as possible. One more breath, and I went under once more.

I slid my wrists below the stump of my leg. My right hand was in front again. I bent over farther and felt for the metal clip. I found it and used my thumb to push in the spring. But with my lungs as full of air as I could manage, my body was too buoyant. I tried to pull myself down with my left hand, but as it was behind my leg, I couldn't find anything to grip. All of this happened in total darkness, with my eyes screwed shut against the sediment-filled water.

I was nearly to the point of blackout.

I tried to pull my body down with my right hand and unclip the metal at the same time.

Could not do it.

As desperately as I wanted oxygen, I blew the stale, used air out of my lungs, hoping my body would settle enough to create some slack. The bubbles brushed against my face. Every cell of my body screamed for oxygen.

Still, I couldn't loosen the clip.

As the white stars of unconsciousness began to fill my vision, I straightened in panic. The handcuff of plastic stopped me short, my right hand in front of my body, my left hand behind. I fought the panic, slid my hands below my stump and up the back of my thighs again. My face broke water, and I flared my nostrils to suck in as much air as possible. If only my mouth were free of the duct tape.

Then it hit me.

I could do it.

Once again, I breathed in lungfuls of sweet air, then plunged down into the darkness of the cold, flowing water. This time, after sliding my wrist beneath the stump, I leaned forward as far as I could. I was able to grab my face with my right hand. I tore at the duct tape and finally grabbed an edge. It pulled away.

I was running short of oxygen again, so I had to go through the process of moving my hands behind my body before I could straighten. This time, however, when I broke the surface of the water, I was able to gasp with an open mouth.

Then I shouted for help.

Again.

And again.

And again.

My throat grew hoarse, but no one came to rescue me. Meanwhile, the water continued its inexorable rise, as the ocean poured itself into the river.

Then came a shock.

As I tried to shout, with my jaw lowered, I took my first mouthful of water. A horrible, salty, foul taste. I shut my mouth and felt the water against my lower lip. How long before it rose high enough to engulf my mouth, then my nostrils?

I tilted my head back and shouted again. And again.

But the wind was blowing into me and my voice was probably lost, unable to reach anyone parked some three or four hundred yards away.

I lost all hope. My death was upon me.

I thought of Angel and Maddie. Abandoned yet again. *Oh, God, protect them,* I prayed. *Find them a good home. A safe home.* I remembered their dance in the moonlight and wept softly at the bitter joy of that memory. I remembered how Angel had served tea in a new dress and how she had curtsied. I remembered the photos of the two Third-World children she had decided to sponsor. How Angel had set aside her wish for a beagle to help those kids. I remembered her glee at fooling Glennifer and Elaine into selling her their ancient telephone. How Maddie clung to her. How Angel loved Maddie more than herself.

In that moment, I realized that God had given me a great gift. Regret. How much more sad to die with nothing to leave behind.

And at that very moment, with Angel and Maddie in mind, I decided if I was going to die, it would not be without a fight. Once more I filled my lungs with air and prepared to bend beneath the water to fight the metal clip that held me prisoner. I ducked, slid my hands beneath my stump, and reached awkwardly for the front of my foot with my right hand.

I had, at the most, forty-five seconds to free myself.

I overextended briefly, and my hand brushed against something that gave me the sense of flapping softly.

It took me a second to realize what it was.

An ear. A human ear.

I almost recoiled, then thought of Miles Ashby. His body

must have dropped into a submerged log or a stump, and it was now pinned in place by the current.

Then I remembered his threat to me in the back of the taxi. Macabre as it was, I clutched his ear and pulled him toward me. I had to fight the current, but this was my final hope and I was not going to let the tide defeat me.

Not yet.

I twisted hard, so my left hand could assist my right hand. I was stooped over badly and working blind.

Twenty seconds of air left?

I pulled him close enough to grab the collar of his suit jacket. Keeping a death grip on it with my left hand, I groped with my right. Down the front of his chest, inside his suit-jacket pocket.

Where I'd seen him replace the switchblade.

Five seconds of air. It took all my willpower not to breathe in the water around me.

My fingers bumped against the hard flatness of the switchblade. Frantically, I dug for it. Closed my fingers around it. Pulled it loose. Then I brought my hands upward and looped them behind me again, still clutching the switchblade. Tilting my head up like a breaching whale, I gasped again. The water threatened to flow into my mouth.

I had one chance and thought rapidly through how I would use it best.

My fingers were numb; I was terrified I would drop the knife. Carefully, very carefully, I managed to unlock the blade. Another lungful of air and I submerged again.

This time, when I worked my right hand beneath the

stump of my leg and in front of my body, I felt with my left hand for the plastic loop around my ankle. I jammed the blade of the knife behind the loop and sawed frantically, not caring how badly I gouged my leg. Finally, when I thought my lungs would explode, the plastic loop snapped. My leg popped loose from the cinder-block anchor.

But I wasn't clear yet.

My body tumbled with the current. I kicked with my free leg. The creek was only twenty feet wide. Could I hit the bank in time with only one leg to propel me?

Then my shoulders hit mud.

I pushed down hard with my good leg. My foot sank slightly, but it still pushed me higher up the bank. Two more pushes and my face was out of the water.

I lay back, heaving and heaving. Once I tried to lift my left leg and slide my hands under it too, but the current threatened to send me tumbling again. So I resorted to the switchblade. With my hands on my chest in case I dropped it, I worked the blade in between my wrists, then slowly sawed back and forth until that bond finally snapped.

With my hands free, I was able to turn and pull myself up the bank. Ahead of me was still a long slow crawl to reach my prosthesis on top of the culvert. Then a walk to a phone booth to call Jubil for help.

I was shaking with chills, covered in mud, and half delirious.

But it was the delirium of elation.

With a profound awareness of and gratitude for just how much God had returned to me.

CHAPTER

28

At the far south of the business end of King Street, tucked between two buildings like a narrow alley, is an unexpected tunnel of promise for foot-weary tourists unfamiliar with this part of Charleston.

The pathway is guarded with a gate that is open during the day, inviting the curious to step farther inside, into the shade of vines covering the walls on both sides. The secret promised is serenity rewarded, for behind the buildings here on King is a lovely and secluded courtyard, adjoined to a church hidden from the street outside.

It was into this solitude that I invited Isabelle Saffron the next morning.

She was prompt. Church bells had echoed the last chimes of ten o'clock when she appeared on the path in her wheelchair pushed by her caretaker. It was a pleasant morning, and I would not have been surprised if he had walked her here from her residence south of Broad.

I was waiting on a bench, drawing in the fragrances of damp vines and molding leaves, marveling at the commonplace. It was, I knew, a result of the euphoria of God's rescuing me from almost certain death, and I hoped I would learn enough from this euphoria to continue to see the world around me with new and unjaded eyes after the sensation faded.

I rose and half bowed as Mrs. Saffron and her caretaker approached.

She dismissed him with a wave, and he turned back to King Street, disappearing down the narrow alley to the busy commercial sector on the other side.

"Mr. Barrett," she said, "I did not expect to hear back from you. And certainly not this quickly."

The wrinkled flesh on her face was folded upon itself. It reminded me that all I had done the previous evening was forestall my own death. With the rising tide, I had seen death's arrival only minutes away before finding a way to postpone it. But in the scheme of eternity, did minutes matter much against years or decades? As philosophers have noted, only the time and manner of a man's death are uncertain. Still, how many of us live with that awareness? How many live preparing for the certain arrival of death?

"Mrs. Saffron," I said. I sat on the bench so we were at eye level. "When we last met, you asked me to find out why your son had been placed in a position where he would die as he did."

On the bench beside me was a file folder. It held roughly two hundred pages of handwritten diary entries.

Those pages were the result of my fear of flying. At the airport in Chicago the day before, I'd had the time to photocopy Anson Hanoway Saffron's diary and drop the copy in an overnight box for Kellie. I'd included the recording of my conversation with the woman who had once lived in Charleston as Victoria Sebastian. I'd only done it because, as with each time I flew, I could not ignore the unreasonable fear that it would be my last flight. With the original of the diary stolen the night before, I was extremely grateful the package had arrived for Kellie at the hospital first thing this morning.

I opened the file folder and found the necessary pages near the bottom of the pile.

"Here's the reason," I said, handing her the pages. "In your son's own words."

Anson Hanoway Saffron sat on a bench in Hampton Park. He was writing poetry by the beam of a fading flashlight when he heard steps. Not the steps of the black, polished boots that belonged to a Citadel cadet's uniform. But the lighter, almost inaudible steps of sneakers. Still, because of a light post on the path, Anson recognized his visitor as a senior cadet.

Anson stood, saluted. He was out of uniform and should not have been.

"At ease," his visitor said. Kindly. "Sit down."

Ethan Osgoode introduced himself, although it was not

necessary. Ethan was well known among the senior cadets. His hair, cut short like all the Citadel's students, was blond. A tall, muscular young man, he carried himself with easy grace. He smiled, showing teeth that had been cared for by expensive orthodontists.

Anson, on the other hand, showed little ease. He protected his closed notebook in his lap with a hand over the top of it.

Ethan sat on the bench beside Anson, leaving a comfortable distance between them.

"I know you're a freshman," Ethan said. "I followed you here. Somehow I doubt you have a pass."

"Do you intend to report me?" When afraid, Anson had a habit of speaking the way he'd write an English essay.

"If other cadets see you, yes. Simply to protect my reputation as a senior. You see, inside the Citadel, I am the perfect cadet. Inside the Citadel, I am an actor. And I am very good at it. It is a role I enjoy. None can defeat me at it. Outside the Citadel . . ." Ethan gave a disarming grin, and Anson relaxed some. "I watched you for a few minutes before I walked up," Ethan said. "I'm curious. What's in your notebook?"

Anson immediately pulled the notebook closer. An unconscious protective act.

"I'm not asking you as a senior cadet," Ethan explained. Another smile. "If I were, you would hand it to me instantly. Or face punishment." His voice softened further. "I'm asking you as someone who could be your friend."

"Friend . . ." Anson was hesitant.

"Outside the Citadel. Where I can be the real me. Inside

the Citadel, where we must be actors each in our roles, we will not be friends. Ever."

Anson did not drop his guard.

Ethan cajoled. "What were you writing? A letter?"

Anson spoke very softly. "Poetry."

Ethan did not laugh as Anson expected. Instead, he smiled more. "I write poetry too. Outside the Citadel. Never inside. Cadets don't write poetry, and inside the Citadel I'm the one cadet who will never lose to anyone. Remember, one person inside, another outside."

"I think I understand." Anson allowed himself a ray of hope. If Ethan wrote poetry—even if it was outside of the Citadel and hidden—perhaps they really could be friends. Even if they couldn't be friends inside, outside it would be worth so much to be able to share his thoughts, speak his heart, vent the unbearable loneliness.

Without waiting for Ethan to ask again, Anson offered the notebook. Ethan took it. Read quietly. And when finished, bowed his head. When he raised it again, there was the shiny track of a single tear on his cheek, barely visible in the dim light cast upon them by the light post farther down the path.

"I knew it," Ethan said. "I watched you over the last week and knew that our souls could be close. It made me want to . . ."

Anson searched Ethan's face during that pause, trying to intuit the meaning of the pause.

"It made me want to protect you," Ethan finally said. "In the way I was protected by an older cadet when I first entered the Citadel."

"Protect me." Anson spoke as if he were trying out the concept.

"As long as you always remember that inside the Citadel we cannot be friends. Ever. Inside the Citadel it will look like I hate you as much as any other knob. Only you would know that when I spit on you, it is part of the act. Just as I knew, when I was a knob and my protector was a senior, that he had to play his part."

"Protect." Anson said it wistfully, his mind filled with the horrors of the stories he'd heard and the hazing he'd already witnessed.

"Protect," Ethan repeated. "Secretly. I could make sure you get hazed lightly. I could warn you of places not to go. There are many ways I could make life much, much easier for you as a freshman, just as my senior did for me. . . ."

Ethan had moved imperceptibly closer.

That's when Anson understood what was being offered. And what would be required of him. That's when the dam of innocence broke and the dark water of repulsion and horror rushed past the crumbling walls of the broken dam.

"No!" Anson stood. "No!"

Without thinking, he swung violently. And outside the Citadel, Anson Hanoway Saffron committed the greatest sin he could have committed inside the Citadel. He struck a senior cadet.

Ethan was an athlete of amazing quickness. Even with such short warning, he was able to pull back. The blow merely grazed his cheekbone.

"That was a mistake," Ethan said. His face twisted with

ugliness. "You will pay the price. And let me warn you, say a word of this, and I will let the entire college know that you were the one who approached me. Who will they believe? A senior cadet on all the sports teams? Or a knob who writes poetry?"

Anson scooped up his notebook and fled.

✛

When Isabelle Saffron finished reading her dead son's hand-written description of the events of that evening, she gave me back the papers. I tucked them in place and closed the folder.

"That night," I said, repeating what Victoria Sebastian had told me in Chicago the day before, "Osgoode returned to the Citadel. He told his three closest friends about it. All of them, of course, were seniors. Most of what Osgoode told them was the truth. Except Osgoode reversed it, said that Anson had begged for protection and promised unnatural favors in exchange for it."

Isabelle sat straight. Her blue eyes seemed to absorb all light as she stared past me.

"The four seniors made a pact that night," I continued, "to rid the Citadel of your son. But without revealing why. They believed that even to hint that your son had such a bent would reflect badly on the honor of the institute. This twisted honor, of course, was Ethan's suggestion. He was terrified that Anson would not only deny any open accusation by Osgoode, but accuse Ethan instead. And Ethan, who had hidden this secret about himself since entering the Citadel, was equally terrified of being smirched even by a counter-accusation."

Still no response from her. To my eyes in this moment, she was not only aged but ageless in the way that weatherworn monuments are ageless.

"Nothing they did could force Anson to leave," I said. "Until that final night."

"They crucified him." Her words came from the depths of her body, a groan of anger and anguish.

"Worse," I said. "He didn't jump from the chair. He was too tough to give in to their hazing. Screws had been removed from the legs. He was murdered."

I watched Isabelle Saffron carefully. She didn't even flinch.

"Ethan Osgoode did it," I said quietly, "out of fear that your son would someday let the world know what happened in Hampton Park."

No reaction.

"This is something you've known for decades, isn't it? You asked me to find out why it was done to your son, but you already knew."

If anything, she became even more still.

"My guess is that Matthew himself told you this. The night he died."

She slowly turned her head. Looked through me with those ice blue eyes. I fought an impulse to shiver.

"I find it revealing that you haven't asked me for the copies of the diary," I said. "I think you came here this morn-ing not to find out about your son but to find out what I knew."

No answer.

"You may have another visitor today," I said. "The original of the diary was stolen from me last night. By a taxi driver. I think you are well acquainted with him. An employee of yours."

No answer. No response.

"How long," I asked, "have you been part of the Sisters of Magdalene? Before the night that Whitman Metiere died at his own masquerade ball?"

She smiled in such a way that suddenly I knew she'd killed him too.

✠

Victoria Sebastian had explained to me in Chicago that her recruitment into the Sisters of Magdalene had begun within months of her marriage to John Sebastian.

Recruits were chosen based on three requirements:

One, wealth.

Two, marriage to a connected husband.

Three, motivation.

Victoria had fit all three, of course. She'd married into wealth, married a connected husband, and was a victim of domestic abuse herself.

The women of the Sisters of Magdalene were often able to shape events by influencing their husbands, and when that didn't work, through intimidation. The yearly gathering took place at the masquerade ball, and occasionally this event also became the night when certain men were intimidated by a ceremony.

Such as the one that John Sebastian had faced.

That night in the coffin, when John Sebastian had smelled his wife's perfume, he had not smelled it on another man. He'd smelled it on her.

✜

"I want to tell you a story," Isabelle Saffron said. "About a girl who lived a sheltered life in a mansion near the waterfront. She grew up with private schools, vacations in Europe, even her own jewelry collection. Then, gradually, all of it began to disappear. Her father's business began to flounder. The vacations ended first, the private school last. In between, the father was reduced to begging his wife and daughter to allow him to sell the jewels he had once given them, piece by piece, as he tried to salvage his business. The daughter did this gladly. She loved her father.

"Still, it wasn't enough. It appeared that all of it would be lost. The business that had once supported the family in such style. The waterfront mansion that had been mortgaged, then remortgaged. The bank was about to foreclose. Can you imagine the humiliation facing this family, one that had once been so wealthy and proud?"

I listened, mesmerized by the powerful cadence of her low voice.

"Then another businessman stepped in. A competitor to the girl's father. The competitor visited the mansion of this girl's family. She was fifteen then, and if predictions were accurate, would in a few years be one of Charleston's most beautiful debutantes in generations. If her family remained in the mansion. This man made the girl's father an offer to lend him money and further help the business by diverting back the business's lost contracts. The fifteen-year-old girl knew this because she was on the other side of the door, listening to every word of the meeting."

Isabelle's hands were in her lap. She shifted them, placing the upper hand beneath the lower hand, then resumed speaking in a voice without passion. "There was one condition to the offer. That the father allow this competitor time alone with the fifteen-year-old girl." Isabelle took her eyes off a distant point and shifted them to mine. "The family business was saved, as was the family mansion. Partly because the father accepted that offer from the rival businessman and the daughter obeyed her father enough to make the one condition possible. And partly because of a life-insurance payment to the family. The father died weeks later. Suicide."

She let me think about that for several moments, then continued. "Imagine what it was like for that daughter to one day discover that the rival businessman had actually been behind all the difficulties that forced her father to almost lose his business. That the rival businessman had done it simply to be able to have time with that once-innocent girl."

I found myself staring at my own hands in my lap.

"Then imagine that this girl, now a woman, grown-up and married into another powerful family, is given the chance to become part of a secret society of women, a society founded to protect other women. And imagine that a time comes when this woman is alone with the man who took her innocence and took her love for her father and drove her father to suicide. Imagine the man is trapped and bound and helpless in an open coffin at midnight. And that the woman who placed him there, with the help of twelve others, has returned to be alone with him."

Isabelle smiled again. A picture of elderly peace. "Imagine, with it dark and quiet as the woman stood over the coffin, how much this woman enjoyed telling the man what she was about to do. Imagine that she placed a cloth in his mouth and pinched his nostrils shut, making his body buck for air, until he was as dead as the father he'd taken from her. Imagine her satisfaction when the man paid the price for what he had taken from her."

Isabelle picked up a cell phone that had been tucked between her leg and her wheelchair. She called for her caretaker to return.

"Good-bye, Mr. Barrett," she said. "Now that I've discovered you have a copy of the diary too, I expect the remaining years of my life will be complicated with legal difficulties."

She wheeled her chair toward King Street, where her caretaker was already walking down the narrow path in our direction.

"I also expect that you, like others," she said, turning her head to me, "will judge my actions harshly. But understand this. Retribution is a consolation that you will never appreciate until something you love more than anything in life is taken from you. Like a father. And a son. Justice was dealt to those who took them."

"You've read the diary then," I said. It must have reached her during the night. Had the taxi driver's blackmail demands been met in the way that Miles Ashby had described to me?

"I've read the diary."

"At the Citadel," I said, "your son's honor and dignity and reputation were all unjustly taken from him, things I believe he would have valued as much as anything else in this life. Despite the injustice, your son found a far more powerful consolation than retribution. We all have that choice. Even you. Now."

Her caretaker arrived and ignored me as he pushed her out of the courtyard and back to her mansion south of Broad. Isabelle Saffron dismissed me with a wave of her hand.

CHAPTER

29

About six weeks later, on a sunny afternoon after school, I stood on a sidewalk near the courthouse with Angel.

"Explain to me a grand jury again," she said.

Instead, I handed her a twenty-dollar bill.

"Nick?"

"You tried to change the subject, so I'm changing it back to the antique business. You might recall that less than thirty seconds ago I asked you about a Web site called Angel's Antiques."

"Asking you about the grand jury is changing the subject? Nick, we're right here. Waiting for some middle-aged white people to come out of the courthouse. A person would think you'd be glad for the opportunity to educate me on the American justice system."

"I'm middle-aged and white, so don't say it like it's an insult. And yes, it's a subject change when I've already explained the grand jury to you three times. So when I ask you about the Web site and hand you twenty dollars, I'm basically conceding defeat. Remember, twenty dollars donated to your sponsored child's Christmas present if you were right about Glennifer and Elaine?"

She took the twenty and gave me a broad smile. "You figured it out, huh?"

A steady stream of overnight packages had been arriving for Angel. Just as she'd been buying a steady stream of antiques. None of which ever made it into our home.

"You mean did I figure out that for the last two months you've been secretly posting their furniture on your Web site, marking it up by 5 percent, and buying those pieces from Glennifer and Elaine when they sell to ship them across the country?"

"Yup. You figured it out."

"When were you going to tell Glennifer and Elaine?"

She shrugged. "Probably tomorrow."

"Because I know about it now?"

"Nick," she said gravely, "that is so unfair." She grinned. "Unfair, but accurate."

"Angel . . ."

"I've kept all the records in a notebook." She spoke seriously again. I noticed she used proper grammar around me and street slang around her friends. "I've kept track of my hours. And all of the proceeds are in a bank account. I was going to give it another month, then give Glennifer and

Elaine a check for how much they would have made off the Web site if they had hired me to do it, less payment to me for my time. To prove to them it works."

"I thought it was something like that. And your profits?"

"Goes to our sponsored kids, Nick. Notice that Maddie points to their pictures on the fridge and says their names now? I taught her that."

The courthouse doors opened. The first of the middle-aged white people began to spill out. I kept an eye on the crowd, looking for a woman whose photo I'd seen in a Chicago luxury high-rise apartment.

"One thing, Angel. Did you have anything to do with the telemarketers? Getting their name on a list or two to make sure they were hassled?"

"Explain to me again the grand jury, Nick. I'm real slow on that kind of stuff, and I'll bet it would help me in school."

I hid a smile. "Why'd you do it, Angel?"

"Gave us a common enemy. So we'd start to join forces."

"Angel, you terrify me."

She put her hand in mine and squeezed. "Thanks. I love it when you say nice things."

I couldn't tell if she was being sarcastic, and I had no chance to explore the issue.

Coming down the steps of the courthouse was a young woman, not quite in her thirties, in a sweater and jeans. Her reddish hair was cut short, and she wore dark-rimmed glasses. She was walking beside her mother.

Sophia Sebastian.

Six weeks earlier, while I'd been in a courtyard off King Street with Isabelle Saffron, Jubil and three other detectives from the Charleston police force had arrived at the Saffron mansion with a warrant to search the premises.

The judge who'd granted the warrant had based it on a single section of the photocopied diary of Anson Hanoway Saffron. The same section that Victoria Sebastian had read with horror and sudden understanding of why Isabelle had asked her to deliver Matthew Pederson by taxi all those years before.

In this section, Anson had described finding ancient embalming equipment and a manual for its use hidden in a corner of the carriage house at the back of the property. He'd asked his mother about it, and she'd joked that if anyone crossed her, they ended up in a coffin beneath the community lodge.

It had been enough of a reference for Victoria to understand the grim truth behind it. Enough for her to decide she wanted out of Charleston, out of the Sisters, and out of an abusive marriage.

It had also been enough for the detectives. In the carriage house they'd discovered the embalming tools.

Along with a yellow taxi and a coffin.

Jones, the man who'd tried to murder me, was inside, ready for burial.

"Hello," I said, with Angel beside me.

From the sidewalk at the courthouse, she and I had

moved slowly toward Victoria and Sophia, waiting for a group
of reporters to finish asking questions.

Victoria Sebastian recognized me immediately and smiled
wanly. "Nick Barrett. The cause of all this."

"This is Angel," I said.

"Pleased to meet you," Angel said, offering a hand to
shake.

"My daughter, Sophia," Victoria said.

"I was hoping to have a moment alone with you," I said
as I shook Sophia's hand.

She looked at her mother, who nodded.

"Angel," I said, "please don't try to sell Victoria any
antiques in the next few minutes."

Sophia followed me down the street until I stopped, well
away from anyone who could overhear us.

"I'm only indulging my curiosity," I told Sophia. "Forgive
me if you think I'm being rude. But you see, someone hired an
agency in Chicago to search for your mother and . . ."

"Yes," she answered simply. "I did."

She spread her hands to take in the scene around us.
A small crowd of people. A television van. Cameramen.
Reporters. "I didn't quite expect this, but I did want the truth.
Without hurting or risking danger for my mother. I grew up
knowing we were running from something but did not know
what or why. In January, when the bodies under the lodge
made national news, I remembered something that happened
when I was a girl. In Searchlight, Nevada."

I nodded. "On the steps. While your mother packed in a
hurry. You heard her speaking to someone about those bodies."

Her silent surprise was enough of an answer. She recovered quickly.

"It was strange in the years after. Mother called me Lizzie, said it was a nickname. But on the school rolls and everywhere else, I had a different name. I was always too afraid to ask why. When I learned about Charleston, it wasn't difficult to discover who my mother was. All I did was go to the newspaper archives. And that's when I learned who I was too. But I decided I didn't dare do anything about it until I knew what Mother was hiding. And if it would finally be safe to reveal our identities." She gave a wry smile and spread her hands again to indicate the scene around us. "And this was the result."

I wondered, too, if she'd been motivated by discovering that her biological father was one of the richest men in Charleston, but I didn't ask. I figured I'd find out later, if and when she pursued her inheritance.

So I simply thanked her. And thought about what I had learned about the faith of a young man named Anson Hanoway Saffron.

✛

Anson's final journal entry was this:

Matthew Pederson stopped me today as I was crossing the parade grounds. He asked if I'd started Bible thumping. He'd heard what I'd told a freshman was the

reason that hazing didn't bother me. Pederson said there
was no room around here for thumping the Bible.

I said that wasn't what I'd done. That someone had
asked why I didn't get mad or afraid or want to quit
with all the abuse heaped on me. And that I'd
answered honestly. There was nothing for me to be
afraid of. I have given myself completely to something far better and far more lasting—a life with
Jesus Christ. A life where this world is not my final
resting place—heaven is. And because of that I can
still hold my head high, even when I'm heaped with
earthly abuses. I said I felt sorry for the seniors who
were really terrible to freshmen, because hatefulness
is a sad way to live.

That's when Pederson lost it on me. He asked if I
was accusing him of being a pitiful human being. Said
that if I was going to put religion ahead of the Citadel,
I didn't belong at the Citadel. That he and his friends
were really going to make sure they got rid of me.

Then he laughed and said that Ethan Osgoode had
figured out a way to make it happen. He said they were
going to find a way to test how much I believed.

Pretty soon, some night they were going to give me
a chance to choose. If I told them I would give up

Jesus, I could be a Citadel cadet and they'd stop bothering me. But if I didn't, it would be my last day at the Citadel.

When that night comes, I hope I can be strong. For him.

Matthew Pederson had read it and been changed.

So had Victoria Sebastian.

And my own faith had been tested and strengthened.

Faith was worth something. But only if there was a price behind it. Like Jesus dying on the cross. Like Anson Hanoway Saffron holding firm to his beliefs, even when he was hazed and then later crucified on the cross in the Citadel gymnasium. Because true faith makes demands. Otherwise it wouldn't be true. Or faith.

"That didn't take long, Nick."

"Didn't expect it to take long, Angel."

"Did you ask that woman out?"

"Angel, I'd never ask someone out without getting your permission first."

The answer seemed to satisfy her. "Good. I think Kellie's definitely got a thing going for you, and I'd hate to see her get hurt."

"Me too." I wasn't about to explain the intricacies of the differences between a friendship and a romance. Or the complications that began when the two started to mix.

Angel and I were walking back to our home, only about five blocks from the courthouse. Living on the peninsula of Charleston is definitely advantageous for someone like me, someone who finds it difficult to walk for more than twenty minutes in any one stretch of time.

"Another question, Nick. Where did Kellie go in your Jeep after she dropped us off at the courthouse?"

"Guess you'll find out when we get home, Angel." I smiled.

"Come on. Give me a hint."

"Think of rabbits," I said.

"Rabbits! What kind of dumb hint is that?"

I smiled again. Kellie had agreed to run an errand for me. We were both trying to pretend that that one moment in the hospital had not happened, the moment she'd reached for me. She, I believed, was pretending because she was proud. Me, because I knew I wanted our friendship to be something more, and I was waiting for the right time to reach back. I hoped I would not have to wait long. She was close to 100 percent recovered; she received the reward for her investigative report, and we both knew she wasn't in a vulnerable position, clutching the nearest support person. It would be good between us; I could sense it.

Kellie had gone to the pet store to get something for Angel.

Rabbits. It was a good enough hint. As in something that loved to chase rabbits. When Angel saw the beagle puppy waiting for her on the front porch, she'd figure it out.

suspense with a mission

request these novels at your favorite bookstore

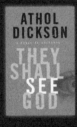

Crown of Thorns   Sigmund Brouwer

Nick Barrett returns in Crown of Thorns, *a compelling psychological thriller that explores the ultimate mercy— God's grace. Readers will be gripped by suspense as Nick unearths a secret hidden beneath Charleston's high society.* (ISBN 0-8423-3038-0 HARDCOVER)

Firefly Blue   Jake Thoene

In this action-packed sequel to Shaiton's Fire, Chapter 16 is called into action when barrels of cyanide are stolen during a truckjacking incident. Experience heart-stopping action as you read this gripping story that could have been ripped from the headlines. (ISBN 0-8423-5362-3 SOFTCOVER)

Blind Sight   James Pence

Thomas Kent is reluctantly drawn into the murderous plot of a dangerous cult as he helps to save the wife and children of an old acquaintance. Enjoy page-turning suspense from this talented new author. (ISBN 0-8423-6575-3 SOFTCOVER)

Into the Nevernight   Anne de Graaf

Award-winning author Anne de Graaf delivers an emotionally gripping story of international intrigue. While vacationing in Africa, Miriam Vree loses everything when a ruthless merce- nary seizes her family. Hear the voices of the refugee children as Miriam discovers eyes to see and a heart that understands. (ISBN 0-8423-5289-9 SOFTCOVER)

for more information on other great Tyndale fiction,
visit www.movingfiction.net

Visit us at movingfiction.net

Check out the latest information on your

favorite fiction authors and upcoming new

books! While you're there, don't forget to

register to receive *Page Turner's Journal*, our

e-newsletter that will keep you up to date

on all of Tyndale's Moving Fiction.

MOVING FICTION ... *leading by example*